SOFIA PETROVNA

Lydia Chukovskaya, who lived in Leningrad during the
Stalinist purges of the 1930s, had numbered most of the
great Russian writers of her day among her friends. She
has been at the centre of a movement to encourage and
promote Russian literature amid a climate of censorship.
This searing novel, *Sofia Petrovna*, which is a synthesis
of the tragic events of the year 1937 written at almost the
very time they were taking place, is to be followed by
the first publication in English of the singular account
of her friendship with the poetess Anna Akhmatova,
Conversations with Akhmatova.

By the same author

CONVERSATIONS WITH AKHMATOVA

Lydia Chukovskaya

SOFIA PETROVNA

Translated from the Russian by

DAVID FLOYD

COLLINS HARVILL
8 Grafton Street, London W1
1989

Collins Harvill
William Collins Sons & Co. Ltd
London · Glasgow · Sydney · Auckland
Toronto · Johannesburg

BRITISH LIBRARY CATALOGUING IN PUBLICATION DATA
Chukovskaya, Lydia Korneeva
Sofia Petrovna.
I. Title II. Floyd, David, 1914–
III. Opustelyi dom. England
891.73'44[F]

ISBN 0-00-271741-7

First published with the title Opustelyi Dom
in New Journal, 1966

First published in English with the title The Deserted House
by Barrie & Rockliff, London, 1967

This revised edition first published in Great Britain by
Collins Harvill 1989
© Lydia Chukovskaya, Magazine Neva, Leningrad, 1988
English translation © William Collins Sons and Co. Ltd 1989

The translation of the Afterword by Eliza Kellogg Klose
is reproduced by permission of Northwestern University Press,
Evanston, Illinois.

Photoset in Linotron Caledonia by
Rowland Phototypesetting Ltd, Bury St Edmunds, Suffolk
Printed and bound in Great Britain by
Hartnolls Ltd, Bodmin, Cornwall

CONTENTS

PREFACE

In 1962 Lydia Chukovskaya wrote a Foreword to her SOFIA
PETROVNA *for publication in Russia. This was not reproduced
by the magazine* NEVA *when it printed her story in its February
1988 issue. The following is a new translation of the Foreword.*

The story now being offered to the reading public was written
twenty-two years ago, in Leningrad in the winter of 1939–40.
In it I tried to record the events that we had just lived through
– my country, my family and myself. I was simply incapable of
not writing, but I cherished no hope at all, of course, of ever
seeing my story in print. It was difficult even to hope that the
school notebook into which I had written a fair copy of the story
would escape destruction and be preserved. To have kept it in
the drawer of my desk would have been risky. But I just couldn't
bring myself to burn it. I regarded it not as a work of literature
so much as the evidence of an eye-witness, which it would be
a crime to destroy.

Then the war broke out. The blockade of Leningrad began
and eventually came to an end. The people who had been taking
care of the notebook perished, but the notebook itself was
saved. Having left Leningrad a month before the outbreak of
war, I spent the years from 1941 to 1944 far from my native
city, and it was only at the end of the war, after a long separation,
that my notebook was miraculously returned to me.

The war ended, Stalin died, and I began ever more frequently to hope for something previously beyond the reach of possibility – that the time would come when my story might see the light of day.

After the speeches that were made at the Twentieth and Twenty-second Congresses of the Soviet Communist Party favouring reform of the present regime and exposing the darker aspects of its past I was more than ever eager to see my story in the hands of the reading public and so serving the cause that seems to me to be of vital importance: for the sake of future generations to help people to understand the causes and the consequences of the tragedy through which the people had lived.

I have no doubt that many writers will take upon themselves the task of describing the 'thirties and that some of them, who dispose of a considerably greater number of facts than I do and who possess a greater ability to analyse and indeed greater literary gifts, will record the main features of the period more fully and in greater detail. For my part, I have tried, within the limits of my resources, to depict only what I observed myself.

But whatever merits future testimonies on the subject may conceivably possess, they will have been written at a different period, separated from 1937 by decades, whereas my story was written immediately after the events had taken place. That is where it differs from works that will deal with the years 1937 and 1938 at some time in the future. It is this that, in my view, gives it a right to claim the reader's attention.

It is for this very reason that I am making no changes, but only omitting a passage that seems no longer relevant. I hope it will sound today like a voice from the past, like a story by an eye-witness who, in the face of powerful attempts to distort the truth, has tried conscientiously to perceive and record what was happening before her eyes.

L.C.
1962

1

After her husband died Sofia Petrovna decided to take a typing
course. She felt she had to get herself some sort of training for
a job: it was going to be some time before Kolya started to earn.
Once he finished school he would certainly have to go on to
college, because his father, Fyodor Ivanovich, would never
have allowed his son to be without higher education. Sofia
Petrovna found it easy to master the typewriter. Moreover she
was a good deal more literate than the young ladies of the day.
She passed out with top marks and quickly found herself a job
in one of the bigger Leningrad publishing houses.

Sofia Petrovna became completely absorbed in her work, so
that after only a month at it she could no longer understand
how she had ever managed without having a job. Not that she
found it all that agreeable to get out of bed on cold mornings to
the light of an electric lamp and to stand shivering waiting for
a tram in a crowd of bleary-eyed, glum-faced people. It was also
true that towards the end of the day her head would start to
ache from the clatter of the typewriters. But, on the other hand,
her work had turned out to be so fascinating and so interesting.
As a girl she had always enjoyed going to school and had cried
whenever she had a cold and was forced to stay at home. In
the same way she had now come to enjoy having a job. Her
conscientious approach to her work was soon noticed and she
was made senior typist and put more or less in charge of the
typing pool. The business of distributing the work, counting up
the pages and lines and trimming the sheets provided Sofia

Petrovna with far more pleasure than working at a typewriter herself. Whenever there was a knock at the little shuttered window she would open it, exchange a few polite words and take in the sheets for typing. They consisted for the most part of accounts, plans, reports, official letters and instructions, but from time to time there would be the manuscript of a work by some modern writer.

"It'll be ready in twenty-five minutes," Sofia Petrovna would say glancing up at the big clock. "In twenty-five minutes exactly. No – no sooner." And she would slam down the window and avoid any argument. After a moment's thought she would give the work to the typist she considered most suitable for it. If the work was handed in by the director's secretary it would be given to the girl who was quickest, most literate and most accurate.

In her youth, on occasions when Fyodor Ivanovich was away for long stretches at a time visiting his patients, she used to dream about having her own dressmaking workshop. Pretty girls would sit bending over flouncing rolls of silk in a large well-lit room, while she would display the latest fashions and engage in genteel conversation with elegant ladies as they were being fitted. Still, a typing business was presumably even better and in a way more important. It often happened now that Sofia Petrovna would be the first person to read a new piece of Soviet writing, while it was still in manuscript – a short story or a novel; and, although Soviet novels and stories struck her as being rather boring, they had so much to say about battles, tractors and factory workshops and so little about love, she did nonetheless feel rather privileged. She now took to putting her greying hair in curlers and adding a little blue to the water when she washed her hair to prevent it from turning yellow.

At work she wore a plain black overall – but trimmed with real old-fashioned lace at the neck – and in her top pocket she'd carry a carefully sharpened pencil: thus she felt she looked businesslike, dependable and at the same time elegant. The typists were just a little afraid of her and even to her face called her a real schoolmistress. But they did her bidding. She aimed to be strict but fair. She used to chat happily during the breaks with those of the girls who took real pains to avoid mistakes. They would discuss such matters as the difficulty of reading the director's handwriting and the fact that lipstick did not suit everybody. But she did not unbend towards girls who typed "repeet" instead of "repeat" or "colectiv" instead of "collective". There was one young woman, Erna Semyonovna, who really got on Sofia Petrovna's nerves. There was a mistake in practically every word she typed; she smoked without any thought for other people; and she kept on talking during work. Erna Semyonovna reminded Sofia Petrovna vaguely of a very cheeky maid who had worked for her family back in the old days, before the Revolution. Known as Fani, she had been rude to Sofia Petrovna and had flirted with Fyodor Ivanovich. Why on earth did people employ such folk?

The typist who most appealed to Sofia Petrovna was Natasha Frolenko, a shy, rather plain girl with a wan complexion. There was never a single mistake in her typing, and the margins and spacing were always amazingly well done. To look at her work you had the impression that it was typed on some special paper and on a better quality machine. But in fact there was nothing special about her paper and typewriter; the whole secret lay in the care she took with her work.

The typists' pool was divided off from the rest of the department by a wooden partition in which there was a small window through which people could speak. There was also a door that was kept permanently locked. At first Sofia Petrovna knew nobody in the publishing house apart from her own typists and the messengers who distributed papers round the building. But she gradually got to know everybody. After a couple of weeks she was stopped in the corridor for a chat with the accountant, a bald, middle-aged man but quite good looking. It turned out

11

that he recognized Sofia Petrovna – some time ago, twenty years back, Fyodor Ivanovich had treated him very successfully for some illness. The accountant enjoyed dinghy-sailing and Western ballroom dancing, and Sofia Petrovna was pleased when he advised her to join their dance club. The director's elderly and very polite secretary began passing the time of day with her, and the head of the personnel department always greeted her. There was also a well-known author, a good-looking man, with grey hair, a beaver fur hat and a monogram on his briefcase, who always turned up at the publishers in his own car. He even asked her on one occasion how she liked the last chapter of his novel. "We writers have long since realized that typists are the fairest judges. The fact is," he said, revealing his evenly spaced false teeth as he smiled, "they give a straight opinion and are not prejudiced, like our comrade critics and editors."

Sofia Petrovna also got to know the Party organizer Timofeyev; he had a game leg and was usually unshaven. He would always frown and stare at the ground when he talked. Sofia Petrovna was a little scared of him. From time to time he would summon Erna Semyonovna to the little window, Sofia Petrovna would open the door, and the caretaker would transport Erna Semyonovna's typewriter from the typing pool to the "special section". Erna Semyonovna would follow in the wake of her machine with her nose in the air: it had been explained to Sofia Petrovna that Erna Semyonovna had been "cleared" to handle secret papers and that the Party organizer summoned her into the special section to type classified Party documents.

Sofia Petrovna very soon knew everybody in the business, by name, by position and by appearance – the clerks, sub-editors, technical editors and messengers. At the end of her first month in the job she saw the director for the first time. His office boasted a fine thick carpet, deep, soft armchairs around his desk and no less than three telephones on the desk top. The director turned out to be a young man, not more than thirty-five, well-built and clean shaven; he wore a grey suit with three badges on the lapel, and he was carrying a fountain pen in his hand. He spoke with Sofia Petrovna for no more than two minutes, during which the telephone rang three times and he spoke into one of them as he lifted the other from its rest. The director himself brought up a chair for her and asked her politely if she would be so kind as to stay behind that evening and work overtime. She would have to choose a typist for the work and dictate a report to her. "I have heard that you are very good at deciphering my frightful handwriting," he said with a smile. Sofia Petrovna left the office flushed with the power she wielded and flattered by the confidence shown in her. A well brought-up young man: he was said to have been an ordinary worker who had come up in the world. His hands were indeed rough as a workman's, but, for the rest . . .

The first general meeting of all the employees of the publishers that Sofia Petrovna attended seemed to her rather boring. The director made a short speech about the Fascists coming to power in Germany and the burning down of the Reichstag, then departed in his Ford. He was followed on the rostrum by the Party organizer, Comrade Timofeyev. He was a bad speaker. His pauses between sentences were so long, it seemed he would never continue. "We have to re-cog-nize . . ." he would say in a monotone and then dry up completely. "Our production plans . . ."

Next to speak was the chairman of the local trade union committee, a plump woman wearing a cameo on her breast. Constantly rubbing and cracking her long fingers, she declared that in view of what had happened they would have to squeeze more work into the working day and launch a merciless campaign against late starters. Then, in hysterical tones, she made a brief announcement about the German Communist leader Thaelmann and advised all the employees to join the International Aid organization. Sofia Petrovna did not really understand what it was all about; she found it boring and would have liked to leave, but feared it was not the right thing to do – she shot an austere glance at a typist who was pushing her way through to the door.

However, the meetings soon ceased to be boring for Sofia Petrovna. At one of them the director, reporting on the fulfilment of the plan, said that achievement of their high production figures depended upon the conscientious and disciplined efforts of every member of the collective, not simply upon the political awareness of the editors and authors but on the cleaners, the messengers and every single typist.

"It has to be admitted," he said, "that the typing pool under the direction of Comrade Lipatova is already performing in an exceptionally efficient manner."

Sofia Petrovna blushed and it was a while before she could bring herself to raise her eyes. When at last she forced herself to look around her, everyone seemed to her to be amazingly kind and good-looking, so that she found herself listening to all the strings of figures with unexpected interest.

2

Sofia Petrovna now spent all her spare time with Natasha Frolenko, though the amount of spare time she had was steadily diminishing. Apart from working overtime it was mainly the frequent meetings of the local committee, on to which Sofia Petrovna was soon co-opted, that took up practically all her evenings. Kolya had ever more frequently to warm up his own supper and used jokingly to refer to Sofia Petrovna as his "mother-cum-social-worker". The local committee gave her the job of collecting the trade union dues. Sofia Petrovna was not altogether clear in her mind for what purpose the trade union existed, but she liked dividing up sheets of paper into columns and recording in them who had paid up for the current month and who hadn't, and she liked sticking in the stamps and delivering faultless accounts to the auditing commission. It also gave her pleasure to know that she could at any moment enter the director's impressive office and remind him with a smile that he owed four months' dues, and that he would, with equal good humour, apologize to the patient comrades of the local committee, pull out his wallet and pay up. She could even, without running any risk, remind the sullen Party organizer of his debts.

At the end of her first year in the job an event of tremendous importance took place in Sofia Petrovna's life. At a general meeting of the whole staff she made a speech on behalf of all the non-party employees of the publishing house. It happened like this. The publishers were awaiting the arrival of some very

15

important comrades from Moscow. The caretaker, a very lively young man with carefully parted hair, like an officer's batman's, spent whole days dashing round the building, carting big picture-frames on his back, and at the most awkward moment let the floor polishers into the typing pool. Then, as she walked down the corridor, Sofia Petrovna was approached by the sullen Party organizer.

"The Party organization, together with the local committee," he said, looking as usual at the floor, "has chosen you to deliver the speech containing our production undertakings on behalf of the non-party activists."

The work piled up enormously just prior to the arrival of the people from Moscow. The typing pool did nothing but turn out all kinds of reports and plans. Practically every evening Sofia Petrovna and Natasha stayed behind working overtime, their typewriters making a hollow sound in the empty room. All around them, in the corridors and offices, it was dark. Sofia Petrovna liked those evenings. Once their work was finished, before leaving the brightly lit room for the darkness of the corridor, she would carry on chatting with Natasha, still sitting at their typewriters. Natasha had very little to say but she was a very good listener.

"Have you noticed that Anna Grigoryevna [that was the chairman of the local trade union committee] always has dirty fingernails?" Sofia Petrovna remarked. "Yet she wears a cameo and waves her hair. It would be better if she used soap on her hands more often . . . Erna Semyonovna gets terribly on my nerves. She's so cheeky . . . And have you noticed, Natasha, that Anna Grigoryevna always has something sarcastic to say about the Party organizer? She doesn't like him a bit . . ."

Having dealt with the chairman of the local committee and the Party organizer, Sofia Petrovna went on to tell Natasha about how she had fallen in love with Fyodor Ivanovich and how Kolya had slipped under the wash tub when he was only six months old. And about what a beautiful child he had been and how people on the street would turn round to admire him. They dressed him all in white – a white coat and a white bonnet.

Natasha seemed to have nothing at all to recount, not a single love affair. "I suppose, with a complexion like that . . ." Sofia Petrovna thought to herself. Natasha's life had consisted of nothing but disaster. Her father, a colonel, had died of a heart attack in 1917. Natasha had then been just five years old. The family's house was taken from them and they were obliged to move in with some paralysed relative. Her mother had been a very spoiled, helpless woman, with the result that they went cruelly short of food and Natasha went out to work almost as soon as she was fifteen. Natasha was now completely on her own: her mother had died of tuberculosis a year or so previously and the elderly relative had died of old age. Natasha was in favour of the Soviet regime, but when she applied to join the young Communist organization she was turned down. "My father was a colonel and a houseowner and, you know how it is, they don't believe that I can be a sincere supporter," Natasha said, screwing up her eyes. "From the Marxist point of view perhaps they are right . . ."

Every time she talked about being rejected she seemed on the brink of tears, and Sofia Petrovna would quickly switch the conversation to another topic.

The great day arrived at last. The portraits of Lenin and Stalin were put into their new frames and brought in personally by the caretaker, while the director's desk was covered with a red cloth. The guests from Moscow – two plump fellows in foreign-made suits with foreign-made ties and foreign fountain pens in their top pockets – sat alongside the director at his desk beneath the portraits and pulled documents out of their tightly packed foreign briefcases. The Party organizer in his Russian shirt and jacket looked quite insignificant alongside them. The busy caretaker and Maria Ivanovna the lift girl kept bringing in trays with tea, sandwiches and fruit which they offered first to the guests and the director and then to everybody present.

Sofia Petrovna was so nervous that she couldn't follow what was being said in the speeches. As though hypnotized she just kept staring at the water moving slightly in a carafe. Then, when the director gave the word, she went up to the desk, turned first of all to the director and the guests, turned away from them, and then stood to one side with her hands holding her belt, as she had been taught in her childhood when she had to recite French poems.

"On behalf of the non-party employees," she said in a shaking voice, and then went on to make all the promises about raising the productivity of labour and everything that she and Natasha had put together and that she had learnt off by heart.

Back home she waited up a long time for Kolya to return so that she could tell him about the meeting. Kolya was then doing his final school exams and was spending every evening with his best friend and comrade, Alik Finkelstein. The two of them worked together. Sofia Petrovna tidied up her room and then went into the kitchen to light up the primus stove.

"It's a pity you don't have a job," she said to the kindly wife of the policeman who was washing dishes. "There is so much happening and that adds so much to life. Especially if your job has something to do with literature."

Kolya turned up at last, hungry and wet through from the first spring rain. Sofia Petrovna put a bowl of cabbage soup in front of him. Sitting opposite Kolya, her elbows on the table, watching him eat, she was just about to tell him about her speechmaking when he said: "Do you realize, Mum, that I am now a member of the young Communist organization: it was confirmed today by the office." Having conveyed this piece of news he switched to another subject without a break, his mouth stuffed full of bread. There was a scandal at his school. "Sasha Yartsev, that stupid, reactionary nitwit . . ." ("Kolya, I don't

like it when you use bad language," Sofia Petrovna broke in.)
"That's not the point. Sasha Yartsev called Alik Finkelstein a
Yid. We decided today at the cell meeting to organize a comrades' court, and do you know who was appointed as public
prosecutor? Me!"

After supper Kolya went straight to bed and Sofia Petrovna
lay down behind her screen while Kolya recited Mayakovsky to
her in the darkness. "Don't you think it's wonderful, Mum?"
And when he had finished reciting, Sofia Petrovna told him
about the meeting. "Mum, you really are terrific," said Kolya
and fell asleep.

3

The summer when Kolya completed his schooling was hot and humid, but Sofia Petrovna was not allowed to take her holiday until the end of July. She had no intention of going out of Leningrad but she spent the whole of July yearning for the time when she would be able to sleep in in the morning and at last do all the housework she never had time to do because of her job. She dreamt of getting away from the constant drumming of the typewriters, of buying Kolya a light overcoat and mending his socks, of paying a visit at last to the graveyard, and of getting a decorator to repaint the door. But when her holiday finally started, it was only on the first day, she found, that there was any pleasure in being on holiday. Out of habit Sofia Petrovna continued to wake up at eight; the decorator repainted the door in half an hour; Fyodor Ivanovich's grave was in perfect order; it took no time at all to buy the overcoat; and Kolya's socks were mended in a couple of evenings. The long, empty days dragged on to the ticking of the clock, the empty chatter in the kitchen and waiting for Kolya to arrive for his supper.

Kolya now spent whole days tucked away in the library: he was studying along with Alik in the hope of being admitted to an engineering college, so that Sofia Petrovna saw very little of him. Natasha Frolenko, poor weary creature – she was standing in for Sofia Petrovna at the office – dropped by occasionally, and Sofia Petrovna would question her eagerly about the director's secretary, the committee chairman's quarrel with the Party organizer, and Erna Semyonovna's spelling mistakes. She also enquired about the discussion that had taken place in the director's office concerning the short story written by that rather agreeable writer . . . "How could anybody possibly fail to like it?" Sofia Petrovna exclaimed, clasping her hands. "It contains such a beautiful description of first love. Just like me and Fyodor Ivanovich."

By now Sofia Petrovna was in complete agreement with Kolya when he argued that women should take up some form of social work. In fact everything that Kolya had to say and everything being written in the newspapers now seemed completely natural, as though they had always written and spoken like that. The only thing that Sofia Petrovna seriously regretted now that Kolya had grown up was the loss of her apartment. They had been forced to squeeze themselves into one room at the time of the famine right at the beginning of the Revolution. The family of the policeman Degtyarenko moved into Fyodor Ivanovich's study and the family of a book-keeper took over the dining room. Sofia Petrovna and Kolya were left with Kolya's former nursery. Kolya had now grown up and really needed a room of his own – he was no longer a child.

"But, Mum, would it be fair for Degtyarenko and his children to have to live in the basement while we occupied a nice apartment? Would that really be fair? Answer me that!" Kolya asked earnestly; and he proceeded to explain to his mother the revolutionary purpose behind the seizure of apartments belonging to the well-to-do.

Sofia Petrovna had to agree with him: it would really not be quite fair. All the same, it was a pity that Degtyarenko's wife was such a slut – even in the corridor you caught the stale smell coming from her room. She seemed scared to open a window. Moreover her twins were already sixteen and still couldn't spell properly. Sofia Petrovna found consolation for the loss of her apartment in the fact that the other occupants had chosen her unanimously to represent them with the authorities. It was as

21

though she had become the mistress in charge of her own apartment. Politely but firmly she spoke to the book-keeper's wife about the suitcases she left standing in the corridor. She worked out how much each family had to pay for electricity with the same care as she devoted to collecting trade union dues at work. She regularly attended meetings of representatives of other apartments and reported back to the other occupants everything the house-manager had said. Her relations with the other occupants were on the whole good. Whenever Degtyarenko's wife was making jam she always asked Sofia to come to the kitchen to taste it to see if it had enough sugar. Degtyarenko's wife often dropped into Sofia Petrovna's room to seek Kolya's advice about what could be done to ensure that the twins didn't have to repeat their second year at school yet again, and to gossip with Sofia Petrovna about the book-keeper's wife who was a nurse.

"I wouldn't like to find myself in her tender care – she would think nothing of despatching you to the other world!" said Degtyarenko's wife.

The book-keeper himself was an elderly man with sunken cheeks and blue veins showing on his hands and nose. He lived in fear of his wife and daughter and he made no noise at all in the apartment. But his daughter Valya, the redhead, upset Sofia Petrovna a great deal by using such expressions as "I'll show 'er" and "I don't give a damn!" The book-keeper's wife, Valya's mother, was a nasty piece of work. She would stand po-faced at her primus stove, nagging away at the policeman's wife for letting her stove smoke or at the twins for not shutting the door properly. She had come from an aristocratic family, sprayed the corridor with eau-de-cologne, wore her spectacles on a chain and spoke in a quiet voice; she scarcely moved her lips but used remarkably coarse expressions. On pay-day Valya would start trying to wheedle money out of her for new shoes.

"Don't get any stupid ideas into your head, you silly cow,"

her mother would say without raising her voice, and Sofia Petrovna would quickly slip into the bathroom so as not to hear any more, to be joined soon by Valya who needed to wash her swollen, tear-stained face and to spit into the washbasin all the obscenities she didn't dare tell her mother to her face.

But apartment 46 was on the whole a happy, quiet apartment, unlike the one above it, number 52, which was the scene of bloody battles practically every weekend. Degtyarenko, half asleep after a long day's work, would be summoned regularly to number 52 to draw up a report, along with the house-manager and the yard cleaner.

Sofia Petrovna's holiday dragged on and on – between her room and the kitchen – and then came to an end, to her great joy. It began to rain more often; near the Winter Garden yellow leaves lay on the ground, to be trampled into the mud under people's heels, and Sofia Petrovna, in rubber overshoes and carrying an umbrella, went off to work again every day, waited for the tram in the morning, and at exactly ten o'clock, with a sigh of relief, hung her number on the board. Once again she was surrounded by the clatter of the typewriters, the rustle of paper and the creaking of the door as it opened and shut. Sofia Petrovna would solemnly hand over to the director's elderly secretary the sheets of paper, carefully stacked and pinned together, smelling of carbon paper. She stuck the stamps into the trade union membership books and discussed in the local committee such questions as the tightening of discipline in the work-place and the improper treatment of a messenger by one of the typists. She continued to be rather afraid of the surly Party organizer, Comrade Timofeyev; and she still did not take to the woman chairman of the local committee who had dirty fingernails. Secretly she adored the director and envied his secretary. They were all people she knew well and to whom she was accustomed, so that she felt at home and confident, not hesitating to criticize the cheeky Erna Semyonovna for all to hear. Why on earth did they keep her on? The question would have to be brought up at the local committee.

Kolya and Alik had finished taking their examinations for the engineering college. Once they had seen their names in the list of successful candidates they decided by way of celebration to fix up a radio receiver in Sofia Petrovna's room. Sofia Petrovna was not very keen on having Kolya and Alik practise their technical skills in her room, but she hoped very much that the radio would cost her a good deal less than an iceboat. When Kolya finished school he had set about building a boat so that in the winter he could go sailing in the Gulf of Finland. He got hold of a book about boat-building, managed to obtain some timber, and introduced all of it along with Alik into the room, with the result that it immediately became impossible, not merely to sweep the floor, but even to move about the room. Because of the timber the dining table was moved back against the wall and the divan moved to the window. The planks of wood lay on the floor in a huge triangle and Sofia Petrovna tripped over them a hundred times a day. But all her complaints were in vain. It was no good her trying to explain to Kolya and Alik that it had become as difficult for her to live in the room as if they had brought an elephant home. They kept planing, measuring, drawing and sawing until they became absolutely convinced that the author of the booklet about iceboats was an ignoramus and that they would never succeed in building a boat from his drawings.

They then meekly sawed up the timber and burnt it in the stove along with the booklet. Then Sofia Petrovna put things back in their places and for a whole week was able to enjoy to the full the space and cleanliness of her home.

At first the radio also brought Sofia Petrovna nothing but trouble. Kolya and Alik cluttered up the room with wires, screws, bolts and pieces of wood, and they would stay up every day to two o'clock in the morning arguing about the merits of one kind of receiver or another. When they had got the receiver finished they would not let Sofia Petrovna listen to anything to the end because they always wanted to tune in first to Norway, then England and so forth. Then they conceived a passion for perfecting the receiver and every evening they would set about rebuilding the set from scratch. Finally Sofia Petrovna took the whole business into her own hands – at which point she discovered that the radio really was a very pleasant invention. She learnt how to switch the receiver on and off, forbade Kolya and Alik to meddle with it, and in the evenings listened to *Faust* or a concert from the Philharmonic Hall.

Natasha Frolenko also came along to listen. She would bring her embroidery work with her and sit by the table. She had very skilful hands: she did beautiful knitting and needlework and she embroidered table napkins and collars. The whole of her room was hung with embroidery, and she had started to embroider a table-cloth for Sofia Petrovna.

On her days off Sofia Petrovna would turn on the radio first thing in the morning. She liked to listen to the serious, confident voice that announced that the Scent Shop No. 4 had taken delivery of a large supply of perfumes and eau-de-cologne or that a new light opera was shortly to have its first appearance. She could never resist making a note of all the telephone numbers, just in case. The only programmes that did not interest her at all were the news bulletins about foreign affairs. Kolya went to some trouble to tell her about the German Fascists, Mussolini and Chiang Kai-shek and she listened to him, but only out of politeness. Sitting on the divan with the newspaper, she would read only the current news stories, a short feature article or the court reports. But a leading article or a report from abroad always sent her to sleep and the paper would fall from her hands and cover her face. Far more than newspapers she liked to read foreign love stories in translation which Natasha brought from the library – books like *The Green Hat* and *Hearts of Three*.

March 8th, 1934, was a great day in Sofia Petrovna's life. That morning a messenger from the publishers brought her a basket of flowers. Among the flowers lay a card with the inscription: "To the non-party member of the staff, Sofia Petrovna Lipatova, congratulations on the Eighth of March. The Party organization and the local committee." She placed the flowers on Kolya's desk, beneath Lenin's collected works and alongside a little bust of Stalin. For the rest of the day she went around with a light heart. She decided not to throw the flowers out when they faded, and made up her mind to dry them and slip them inside a book to remind her of that day.

4

Sofia Petrovna had now been in her job for more than two years. Her pay had been raised from 250 to 375 rubles a month. Kolya and Alik were still students, but they were also earning quite well as draughtsmen. For Sofia Petrovna's birthday Kolya bought her with his own money a little tea service – milk jug, teapot, sugar bowl and three cups. Sofia Petrovna did not like the pattern on the service very much – red squares on a yellow background. She would rather have had flowers. But the china was delicate and of good quality, and did it really matter? It was a present from her son.

Her son had become a very good-looking young man – grey eyes, black eyebrows, tall and full of confidence, as relaxed and happy as Fyodor Ivanovich had never been even in his very best years. Kolya always had a sort of military bearing, was always well turned out and alert. Sofia Petrovna eyed him with tenderness and constant concern, rejoicing and yet fearing to rejoice. He was a handsome boy and very fit; he neither drank nor smoked; he was a dutiful son and a loyal young Communist. Alik was also, of course, a polite young man and hard working, but could you compare him with Kolya? His father was a bookbinder living with a large family in Vinnitsa and in some poverty. Since his early years Alik had been living in Leningrad with an aunt who, apparently, did not bother very much with him: the elbows of his jacket were patched and his boots were badly worn. He was frail and small for his age. And he certainly didn't have Kolya's brains.

One thought was constantly worrying Sofia Petrovna: Kolya was already twenty-one and he still did not have his own room. Was she not interfering with Kolya's private life by her constant presence?

"It seems to me that Kolya must have fallen in love with someone there at the college," she framed the question to Alik very carefully. "Who is she? What's her name? How old is she? Is she a good student? Who are her parents?"

Alik dodged the questions, however, and the look in his eyes made it clear that he was not going to tell on Kolya. Sofia Petrovna succeeded only in extracting the girl's name – Nata. But it didn't matter what her name was or whether it was a serious love affair or just a passing fancy, a young man of his years needed in any case to have a separate room. Sofia Petrovna shared her concern with Natasha, who listened to her in silence and then said with a blush: "Yes . . . certainly . . . of course . . . Nikolai Fyodorovich would be better off in a separate room . . . but still . . . I am living alone . . . without my mother . . . and what of it? It's all right." Natasha broke off and fell silent, and Sofia Petrovna did not really grasp what she was trying to say.

Sofia Petrovna pondered the question from all angles, trying to work out how she could exchange one room for two, and she even started putting money away in the savings bank so as to have a deposit ready if necessary. But the question of a separate room for Kolya unexpectedly lost its urgency – the two top students, Nikolai Lipatov and Aleksandr Finkelstein were chosen to be sent as skilled engineers to Sverdlovsk to work in the "Uralmash" factory. Sverdlovsk was short of trained engineers. The college had agreed to let them finish their studies by correspondence.

"Don't worry, Mum," Kolya said, placing his big hand over Sofia Petrovna's little one. "Don't worry. Alik and I will live well there. We have been promised a room in the hostel, and

Sverdlovsk isn't so far away. You will get to us somehow or other and, do you know what? – you can send us parcels."

From that day on, when she returned from work, Sofia Petrovna immediately set about sorting out Kolya's underwear, sewing, darning and ironing. She sent Fyodor Ivanovich's old suitcase to be mended. That spring morning when Fyodor Ivanovich and she had bought the suitcase in the Guards Society shop now seemed so utterly far away, like some unreal morning in some unreal life. She studied with amazement a page from *Niva*, a magazine which had been stuck in the case to strengthen it: she was struck by a picture of a woman with a long dress and a deep décolleté and a tall hair-do. Such were the fashions in those days.

Kolya's departure worried and distressed Sofia Petrovna, but she had to admire the skill and precision with which he packed his books and the big notebooks full of his very legible writing. He sewed his young Communist membership card into his belt himself. The day of his departure was always a week away, and then suddenly it was the next day.

"Kolya, are you ready – Kolya?" Alik Finkelstein asked as he entered the room in the morning, a small figure, with a big head and big ears. "What's going on?"

His new tunic did not fit very well at the back and his shirt collar curled up. Kolya strode determinedly across to his case and lifted it as easily as if it had been empty. On the way to the railway station he made light of carrying his case, while poor Alik could hardly drag his little case along as he puffed and panted, wiping the sweat from his brow with the sleeve of his tunic. With his short legs and big head he looked to Sofia Petrovna like a comic character in a cartoon film. Alik's aunt had not turned up at the station to see him off, of course, so the three of them, Kolya, Sofia Petrovna and Alik, strode solemnly up and down the platform in the damp mist that hung over the station. Kolya and Alik had a lively discussion on the relative merits of the Fiat and the Packard – which car was the lighter and better built. And with only five minutes left before the train's departure Sofia Petrovna remembered that she had not told the boys about the danger of meeting thieves on the journey or about dealing with their laundry. When they handed their laundry in to be washed they were to count it and make a note of it. And they were on no account to eat salads in restaurants: they were often left over from the day before and were not fresh, so that you could easily go down with typhoid. She then led Alik away to one side and gripped him by the shoulder.

"Alik, my dear boy," she said, "please take care of Kolya for me, like a good friend."

Alik looked at her through his glasses with his big, kindly eyes.

"That's no trouble at all. Of course I will keep an eye on Nikolai. What do you think?"

It was time to board the train. Kolya and Alik soon appeared at the window of their compartment – Kolya looking very tall, Alik coming only up to his shoulder. Kolya was saying something to Sofia Petrovna but nothing could be heard through the glass. Then he burst out laughing, took off his cap and cast an excited, happy glance round the compartment. Alik tried to communicate with Sofia Petrovna with his fingers. She made out the word "Don't" and indicated that she had understood – "Don't worry". Goodness, they were really only children!

A minute later she was walking back along the platform, alone in a crowd of people, faster and faster, not looking where she was going, wiping away her tears with her fingers.

5

After Kolya's departure Sofia Petrovna spent less and less time at home. There was always plenty of overtime to do at the office, so she stayed on working practically every evening, and that enabled her to save up to buy Kolya a suit – a young engineer had to be well dressed.

On her free evenings she would take Natasha home with her for a cup of tea. They would drop into the shop on the corner and choose a couple of pastries. Sofia Petrovna would make the tea in the teapot with the little squares and would then switch on the radio. Natasha would bring her embroidery with her. She had recently, on Sofia Petrovna's advice, been dutifully drinking brewer's yeast, but her complexion had not improved.

One of those evenings, as she was leaving Sofia Petrovna to go home, Natasha suddenly asked if she might have the latest photograph of Kolya.

"Otherwise all I've got in my room is a picture of my mother and no one else," she explained.

Sofia Petrovna presented her with a picture of Kolya in a collar and tie, looking very handsome and alert. The photographer had succeeded in catching his smile surprisingly well.

On one occasion, as they were returning from work they slipped into a cinema, and from then on the cinema became their favourite form of entertainment. They were both very fond of films of airmen and frontier guards. Those good-looking pilots performing great deeds of valour reminded Sofia Petrovna of Kolya. She liked the new songs accompanying the films, especially "Thanks, my heart!" and "If your country tells you – be a hero", and she liked the word "Motherland". That word, written with a capital letter, gave her a feeling of warmth and solemnity. And when the best pilot or the most courageous frontier guard was brought down by an enemy bullet Sofia Petrovna would grip Natasha's hand, just as in her younger days she had gripped Fyodor Ivanovich's hand when Vera Kholodnaya had whipped out a little lady's revolver from her big muff and, raising it slowly, aimed it at the head of the villain.

Natasha applied again to join the young Communist organization, and again she was not accepted. Sofia Petrovna could well understand Natasha's disappointment – the poor girl was in such need of company. And why, after all, did they not accept her? She was hardworking and totally devoted to the Soviet regime. For one thing, she was an excellent worker, in fact the best. Moreover, she was politically literate – that was the second thing. She was not like Sofia Petrovna; she would not let a day pass without reading *Pravda* from beginning to end. Natasha understood the situation no worse than Kolya and Alik, both the international situation and the achievements of the five-year plan. She was terribly concerned when the *Chelyuskin* was crushed in the ice – she couldn't tear herself away from the radio. She cut out pictures of Captain Voronin, Schmidt's camp and the pilots from all the papers. When the announcement came about the first people to be rescued she wept as she sat at her typewriter, the tears dropped on the paper and in her happiness she ruined a couple of sheets. "They certainly will not allow people to perish," she kept repeating, wiping away her tears. She was such a sincere, warm-hearted girl, yet she had again been turned down for the young Communists. It was unjust. Sofia Petrovna even wrote to Kolya about the injustice visited upon Natasha. But Kolya replied that injustice was a class concept and that vigilance was essential. After all, Natasha was from a bourgeois land-owning family. The vile Fascist hirelings who had killed Comrade Kirov had not yet been thoroughly rooted out from the country. Class battles were still going on, and that was why there had to be the strictest check on all admissions to the Party and to the young Communist organization. But, he added, in a few years Natasha would probably be admitted and he strongly advised her to study the works of Lenin, Stalin, Marx and Engels.

"In a few years!" said Natasha with a bitter smile. "Nikolai Fyodorovich forgets that I'm almost twenty-four."

"Then they'll take you straight into the Party," Sofia Petrovna said by way of consolation. "And what's twenty-four anyway? Just your first youth."

Natasha made no reply, but when she left for home that evening she took with her a volume of Kolya's Lenin.

Letters arrived regularly from Kolya, every weekend. He was such a fine son, not to forget that his mother worried about him, though he must have plenty of other demands on his time. When she returned home from work Sofia Petrovna would take her key out of her handbag when she was still at the bottom of the stairs; she would go quickly up to the fourth floor where, still out of breath, she would open the blue post-box. A letter in a yellow envelope would be waiting for her. Without taking off her coat she would sit at the window and unfold the carefully folded pages, torn from a notebook.

"Hello, Mum!" – every letter began in the same way – "I hope you're well. I am too. The output of our factory for the last week has reached . . ." They were long letters but they contained more and more about the factory, and the growth of the Stakhanov movement, but not a word about himself or his life. "Just imagine," Kolya wrote in his first letter, "the worm gears, the lathes and even the broaches – everything here is imported from abroad and we have to pay the capitalists in gold for everything because we can't learn to make the things ourselves." But it was not the lathes that Sofia Petrovna was interested in. She would have liked to know what he and Alik were eating and whether they had found an honest laundry-woman. Did they have enough money? And when did they find time to study? At night? Kolya provided only very cursory, incoherent replies to such questions. Sofia Petrovna was so keen to have some idea of their room and how they lived and ate that, at Natasha's suggestion, she wrote a letter to Alik.

The reply came in a few days.

"Dear Sofia Petrovna," Alik wrote. "Forgive my cheekiness, but you have no need at all to worry about Kolya's health. We eat quite well. In the evening I buy some sausage and in the morning I fry it in butter. We have our midday meal at the canteen – three courses, very good. We have decided to use the jam you sent us only with our evening cup of tea, and in that way it will last us a long time. I also make a list of the laundry when I give it to the laundress. We have set aside a special period each day for our studies. You can trust me completely: I do everything for Nikolai as his friend and comrade and try to help him in every way."

The letter ended with these words:

"Nikolai is making good progress with the development of a new method of manufacturing Fellows gear-cutters in our tool workshop. People in the factory's Party committee describe him as our rising eagle."

He should, of course, have said "rising star" and not "eagle", and Sofia Petrovna hadn't the slightest idea what a Fellows gear-cutter was. Nevertheless Alik's words filled her heart with pride and admiration.

Sofia Petrovna put Kolya's letters away carefully in a box beneath her writing paper, which was where she kept the letters Fyodor Ivanovich had written to her when they were courting, photographs of Kolya as a small boy and a picture of the little baby Karina born aboard the *Chelyuskin*. Sofia Petrovna added Alik's letter to her collection. She felt a certain affection for

Alik: he was certainly devoted to Kolya and understood him so well.

One day, ten months or so after Kolya's departure, Sofia Petrovna received in the post a large plywood box. It was from Sverdlovsk, from Kolya. And it was so heavy that the postman had difficulty in carrying it up to her room and demanded a rouble tip. "A sewing machine?" Sofia Petrovna wondered. "Wouldn't that be fine!" She had sold hers when times were bad. The postman departed and Sofia Petrovna took a hammer and chisel to open up the box. Inside was a strange black metal object, carefully packed in shavings. It wasn't exactly a wheel, and it wasn't a drill, there was no telling what it was. Finally Sofia Petrovna found on the back of the mysterious object a label with Kolya's writing on it: "Dear Mother, I am sending you the first gear-wheel cut by a Fellows cutter made in our factory by my method." With a laugh Sofia Petrovna gave the gear-wheel a pat and, with some difficulty, carried it across to the window sill. Every time she glanced at it it made her feel happy.

A few days later, in the morning, when Sofia Petrovna was drinking up her tea, hurrying off to work, Natasha suddenly burst into her room. Her hair was wet from the snow and in great disorder and one of her shoes was unlaced. She held out to Sofia Petrovna a rather wet newspaper.

"Look . . . I just bought it at the corner . . . I was reading it when suddenly I came across Nikolai Fyodorovich – Kolya."

There on the front page of *Pravda* Sofia Petrovna saw Kolya's smiling face and fine teeth. He looked different and rather older in the picture, but there could be no doubt about it – it was her son, Kolya. The caption beneath the picture said:

"Eager to increase production, the young Communist Nikolai Lipatov has developed a new method of making Fellows gear-cutters at the Urals engineering plant."

Natasha embraced Sofia Petrovna and kissed her on the cheek.

"My dear Sofia Petrovna," she said pleadingly. "Please let's send him a telegram."

Sofia Petrovna had never seen Natasha in such a state of excitement. But her own hands were shaking and she just couldn't find her briefcase. They composed the telegram at work in the lunch break and despatched it after work. Everybody was congratulating Sofia Petrovna; at work even Erna Semyonovna congratulated her on having such a son, and at home even the nurse did the same. That evening as she went to bed, happy and tired, Sofia Petrovna realized for the first time that Natasha was probably in love with Kolya. How was it that she hadn't guessed it before? She was a good girl, well brought up and hardworking, but she was so plain, and she was older than Kolya. As she dozed off Sofia Petrovna tried to imagine the sort of girl with whom Kolya would fall in love and become his wife: tall, fresh-looking, with pink cheeks, bright eyes and fair hair, looking very much like an English young lady but with a KIM badge on her breast. Nata? No, Svetlana would be better. Or Lyudmila – Milochka.

6

The New Year – 1937 – was approaching. The local committee decided to put up a fir-tree for the children of people working at the publishers. The task of organizing the party was entrusted to Sofia Petrovna, who co-opted Natasha as her assistant and the work went ahead swimmingly. They phoned around to the employees' homes to learn the names and ages of the children; they typed out the invitations; they rushed around the shops buying up sweets and cakes and decorations for the tree; and they ran themselves off their feet looking for artificial snow. The most important thing, and the most difficult, was to decide which child should have which gift so as to stay within the budget and still see to it that everyone was satisfied. Sofia Petrovna and Natasha even had a bit of a quarrel over what the director's little girl should have. Sofia Petrovna wanted to buy her a big doll, rather bigger than the ones for the other girls, but Natasha thought that would be tactless. They finally came to terms on a pretty little tin whistle with a fluffy bobble on it.

At last all that remained was to buy the fir-tree. They bought a really tall one that reached right up to the ceiling and had long spreading branches. The day of the party, Natasha, Sofia Petrovna and Maria Ivanovna the lift-girl decorated the tree from early morning till two o'clock in the afternoon. Maria Ivanovna amused them with her stories about the director's wife; she always referred to the director in the third person plural, as in pre-revolutionary days. She also presented Natasha and Sofia Petrovna with balloons, crackers, toy post-boxes and little silver boats which Natasha and Sofia Petrovna hung on the tree. Sofia Petrovna's legs soon gave in and she sat in an armchair preparing little bags of sweets with a note inside saying "Thank you Comrade Stalin for our happy childhood". Natasha went on decorating the tree on her own. She had very clever hands and had unlimited good taste – she attached the Santa Claus very effectively. Then Sofia Petrovna stuck a picture of the young Lenin with curly hair in the middle of a big five-pointed star. Natasha fixed the star to the top of the tree and everything was ready. They took from the wall a full-length picture of Stalin and replaced it with another one in which Stalin was sitting with a little girl on his lap. It was Sofia Petrovna's favourite picture of Stalin.

Three o'clock. It was time to go home for a little rest and a bite to eat, and then to change for the party.

The party was a great success. All the children turned up and most of the mothers and fathers too. The director's wife did not come but the director himself did and brought with him his little girl, an adorable child with fair curly hair. The children were delighted with their presents, the parents were loud in their admiration for the fir-tree. Anna Grigoryevna, the chairman of the local committee, was the only one to take offence, because her son had received a drum and not tin soldiers like the son of the Party organizer: the soldiers were more expensive. She came in a green silk dress with even a plunging neckline. Her son, a lanky, rather unpleasant child, whistled, thumped the drum with his fist to show off and then broke it. But all the others were satisfied. The director's daughter never stopped blowing her whistle, hopping about between her father's legs, resting her little pudgy hand on his knee and throwing her head back so as to see the fir-tree properly.

Sofia Petrovna felt she was to be the real mistress of the occasion. She wound up the gramophone, switched on the radio and indicated to the lift-girl by a glance who was to be offered the cakes and sweetmeats. She was sorry for Natasha, who stood back shyly against the wall, looking so pale and grey in the smart new blouse she had embroidered herself. The director bent down and led his little girl around the tree and startled her with Santa Claus. Sofia Petrovna found the scene very touching: she wanted Kolya to be like the director in every respect. Who could tell, perhaps in a couple of years she too would have a sweet little grand-daughter like that. Or a grandson. She would persuade Kolya to call a grandson Vladlen, which was such an attractive name, and a grand-daughter Ninel, an elegant name that looked French but spelt Lenin if you read it backwards.

At last Sofia Petrovna, exhausted by her efforts, sank down into an armchair. It was time to go home – she felt her migraine coming on. But then the imposing accountant came up to her and, bending over politely, passed on a strange piece of news: a large number of doctors had been arrested in the city. The accountant was acquainted personally with all the city's medical luminaries: his eczema had not responded to anyone's treatment – Fyodor Ivanovich alone had found how to cure it. ("There was a real doctor for you! The others keep on giving out prescriptions, rubbing in some ointment and getting nowhere . . .") Among the people who had been arrested the accountant mentioned Doctor Kiparisov, who had been at medical school with Fyodor Ivanovich and was Kolya's godfather.

"What? Doctor Kiparisov? Impossible! What happened? Surely not another . . . accident?" Sofia Petrovna asked, reluctant to pronounce the word "murder".

The accountant glanced upwards and walked away, for some reason or other on tiptoes. Two years previously, following the murder of Kirov (those had been pretty grim days, with soldiers patrolling the streets . . . and when Comrade Stalin had come to Leningrad the square in front of the station had been cordoned off by the army, the streets and side streets closed – you couldn't get through on foot or by car), after Kirov's murder there had also been many arrests, but at the outset they were detaining only some oppositionists and then some former upper-class people and aristocrats. But now doctors were being arrested. Following the murder of Kirov a very old friend of Sofia Petrovna's with whom she had been at school, a Madame Nezhentseva, had been deported because of her aristocratic origins. Sofia Petrovna was at a loss to imagine what connection Madame Nezhentseva could have had with the murder. She had taught French in school and lived as everybody else lived. But Kolya explained that it was essential to rid Leningrad of all unreliable elements. "And what sort of a person, when you come to think of it, was your Madame Nezhentseva? Don't you remember, mother, that she didn't recognize Mayakovsky as a poet and was always saying that everything had been cheaper in the old days. She was not a Soviet person . . ." All right, but what about the doctors? What wrong have they done? Just think of it – Ivan Ignatyevich Kiparisov. Such a highly respected doctor!

The children were crowding noisily into the cloakroom and Sofia Petrovna, as the hostess, was helping the parents to find their clothes and footwear. Carrying his daughter, the director came up to her to take his leave and to thank the committee for a wonderful party.

"I saw a picture of your son in *Pravda*," he said, smiling. "We have a fine younger generation growing up."

Sofia Petrovna looked at him with something like adoration and wanted to say that he had no right at all to talk about a new generation taking over. What was it to be thirty-five? His first youth. But she didn't dare. He dressed his little girl and tied a white fluffy scarf over her fur coat. He seemed to be able to do everything. His wife could let him look after the child without the slightest worry. He was obviously an excellent family man.

7

There was nothing in the papers about the arrest of the doctors or about Doctor Kiparisov. Sofia Petrovna was intending to call on Madame Kiparisova but she just couldn't bring herself to go there. She had no time and moreover she felt rather awkward about it. It was about three years since she had met Kiparisova and it would seem odd if she suddenly dropped in for no apparent reason.

In January the newspapers began to print articles about a new trial due to take place. The trial of Kamenev and Zinoviev came as a shock to Sofia Petrovna but, with her lack of interest in the newspapers, she did not follow the trial day by day. But now Natasha persuaded her to read the papers and they began reading reports of the trial every day. Everybody around her kept talking about Fascist spies and terrorists and arrests. It was hardly credible – the scoundrels had intended to murder our beloved Stalin. It was they apparently who had murdered Kirov. They had organized explosions in mines. They had derailed trains. And they had their own people posted in practically every factory and office.

One of the typists in the pool who had just returned from a holiday home told of a young engineer who had occupied the room next to hers and with whom she had on occasion gone strolling in the park. One night a car had driven up suddenly and the engineer had been arrested: he had turned out to be a wrecker. And he had looked such a nice chap – you just couldn't tell.

In Sofia Petrovna's house, in apartment 45, just opposite, there was also an arrest – a Communist of some kind. A red seal was put on the door of his room. Sofia Petrovna was told about this by the house-manager.

In the evenings Sofia Petrovna would put on her spectacles – she had recently become long-sighted – and read the newspaper aloud to Natasha. The table-cloth was already finished and Natasha was now embroidering a cover for Sofia Petrovna's bed. They talked about Kolya and how upset he must be at the present time. And not only Kolya – all decent people were indignant. After all, the trains that the wreckers derailed could have little children in them! What heartlessness! What monsters! No wonder the Trotskyists were closely connected with the Gestapo; they were really no better than the Fascists who were killing children in Spain. And was it really possible that Doctor Kiparisov had been involved in such a gang of rogues? He had often been invited to join in a consultation with Fyodor Ivanovich, after which Fyodor would bring him home for a cup of tea and a chat. Sofia Petrovna had seen him quite close, as close as she was to Natasha now. And he had joined a gang of bandits! Who would have expected that? Such a highly re-spected old man.

One evening, when they had read the list of offences commit-ted by the accused and had listened to the same list read out over the radio, the two women had such a clear vision of the broken legs and arms and the piles of mangled corpses that Sofia Petrovna was afraid to be on her own in her room and Natasha was scared to walk home alone. That night Natasha slept on Sofia Petrovna's divan.

Everywhere, in all the factories and offices meetings were called, and the publishing house also held a meeting about the trial. The chairman of the local committee went round all the rooms and warned employees that, if there were some irresponsible people who did not want to attend the meeting, they should bear in mind that the main entrance was locked. Every single employee turned up at the meeting, even people working in the editorial department who usually stayed away. The director spoke first, setting out briefly, unemotionally and precisely what had been reported in the newspapers. He was followed by the Party organizer, Comrade Timofeyev. Halting after every couple of words, he said that enemies of the people were active everywhere, that they could even penetrate into the publishing house and that therefore all honest employees must continually raise their level of vigilance. The floor was then taken by the chairman of the local committee, Anna Grigoryevna.

"Comrades!" she said, lowering her eyelids and remaining silent for a moment. "Comrades!" now clenching her hands with their thin fingers and long nails. "The foul enemy has reached out with his filthy paws into our establishment too." Everybody froze. The cameo rose and fell on Anna Grigoryevna's ample bosom. "The arrest took place last night of the former head of our printing works, now exposed as the enemy of the people, Gerasimov. He turned out to be the nephew of the Moscow Gerasimov who was exposed a month ago. Through the slackness of our Party organization, which suffers from what Comrade Stalin described so accurately as the idiotic disease of complacency, Gerasimov continued to 'work', if one can use the word, in our printing works even after the exposure of his uncle, the Moscow Gerasimov."

She sat down. Her bosom rose and fell.

"Any questions?" enquired the director, who had taken the chair at the meeting.

"But what did they do . . . in the printing works?" Natasha asked hesitantly.

The director invited the chairman of the committee to reply.

"What did they do?" she repeated in a high-pitched voice, rising from her seat. "It seems to me, Comrade Frolenko, that

I explained, clearly and in plain Russian, that our former head of the printing works Gerasimov had turned out to be the nephew of the other, Moscow Gerasimov. He remained in daily contact with his uncle . . . disorganized the Stakhanov movement in the works . . . failed to carry out the plan . . . on instructions from his relative and on account of the criminally sloppy behaviour of the Party organization."

Natasha had no more questions.

When she returned home from the meeting Sofia Petrovna sat down to write to Kolya. She told him that enemies had been discovered in their printing works. What was happening in the Uralmash? Was everything all right? As an honest young Communist Kolya had to be vigilant.

At the publishers there was no mistaking the strange feeling of unease that prevailed. The director was summoned every day to Party headquarters. The melancholy Party organizer kept coming into the office, opening the door with his own special key and summoning Erna Semyonovna to the special section. The polite accountant, who appeared to have a way of knowing everything that was going on, told Sofia Petrovna that the Party organization was now meeting every evening.

"The poor dears are quarrelling," he said with a meaningful grin. "Anna Grigoryevna accuses the Party organizer of being responsible for everything, and the Party organizer accuses the director. As far as I can gather, there's going to be a change of management."

"What are they accusing each other of?" Sofia Petrovna asked.

"Oh, they just can't agree which one of them overlooked Gerasimov."

Sofia Petrovna could make no sense of any of it and left the office that day in a vague state of alarm. As she was walking home she noticed a tall, elderly woman with a scarf round her hat, in felt boots and galoshes and a walking stick in her hand. As she walked along the old lady used her stick to avoid a slippery footing. Her face seemed familiar to Sofia Petrovna. Yes, it was Kiparisova! Could it really be her? God, how she had changed!

"Maria Erastovna!" Sofia Petrovna called out to her.

Kiparisova stopped, raised her large dark eyes and, with some difficulty, made the effort to give a smile of welcome.

"Hello, Sofia Petrovna. It's years since we met. Your little boy has no doubt already grown up?" She stood there, holding Sofia Petrovna by the hand but not looking her in the face – her huge dismayed eyes darted in every direction.

"Maria Erastovna," Sofia Petrovna said with real feeling. "I am so glad to have met you. I have heard you have had some difficulties . . . with Ivan Ignatyevich . . . Listen, we after all are good friends. Ivan Ignatyevich was godfather to Kolya . . . of course that doesn't count nowadays, but you and I are old people. Tell me, is Ivan Ignatyevich accused of something serious? Surely there can't be any real foundation for those charges? I am simply unable, quite unable to believe it. Such a wonderful and such a highly respected doctor. My husband always had the greatest respect for him and rated him above himself as a clinical physician."

"Ivan Ignatyevich has committed no offence against the Soviet regime," Kiparisova said gloomily.

"That's what I thought!" exclaimed Sofia Petrovna. "I didn't doubt it for a minute and said as much to everybody."

Kiparisova looked at her with her huge dark eyes.

"Goodbye, Sofia Petrovna," she said without a smile.

"When Ivan Ignatyevich returns ask me for a meal," Sofia Petrovna said. "But why on earth are you so distressed? If Ivan Ignatyevich is not guilty of anything, everything will be all right. In our country nothing can happen to an honest man. It's just a misunderstanding. You will see – just be brave. Come and have a cup of tea with me some time."

"Surely I haven't aged the way she has?" Sofia Petrovna

thought to herself. Her face so drained and full of wrinkles. No, impossible – I don't look like that yet. She has simply let herself go to pieces – going out in felt boots, a stick and a scarf. It's very important for a woman not to let herself go and to take care of herself. Who wears felt boots nowadays? This is not 1918. She looks at least sixty-five when she can't be more than fifty . . . It's a good thing Kiparisov isn't guilty of anything. Of all people a wife must know. It's as I thought – just a misunderstanding, nothing more.

8

Next day the typing pool was working fast to finish the half-yearly report. They all knew that late that night the director was leaving for Moscow by the fast train to deliver his report on the work of the publishing house to the Press Department of the Central Committee of the Party. Sofia Petrovna urged the typists to work faster. Natasha worked right through her lunch break.

By three o'clock four copies of the report lay before Sofia Petrovna who sorted them out and clipped them together carefully.

But the director's secretary did not come to collect the report, so Sofia Petrovna decided to take it to his office herself. At the half-open door of the director's office she bumped into the Party organizer.

"You can't go in there!" he told her and without further greeting he went off limping to another room. He seemed to be in a terrible state.

Sofia Petrovna glanced round the half-open door. There was a strange man on his knees at the desk pulling out papers. There were papers scattered all over the carpet in the office.

"At what time will Comrade Zakharov be here today?" Sofia Petrovna asked an elderly secretary.

"He's been arrested," the secretary replied voicelessly, moving only her lips. "Last night."

Her lips were quite blue.

Sofia Petrovna took the report back to the pool. When she

reached the door of the office she felt her knees giving way beneath her. The noise of the typewriters deafened her. Did they know already or not? They were tapping away as though nothing had happened. If she had been told that the director had died she would have been less upset. She sat at her usual place and began without thinking to remove the clips from the bundles of paper.

At one point Timofeyev came in, opening the door with his private key. Sofia Petrovna noticed for the first time that, despite his lameness, the Party organizer held himself erect and walked with a sure step. She offered a nervous apology when he accidentally knocked against her shoulder as he passed.

At half past four the bell rang at last. Sofia Petrovna went silently down the stairs, put on her outdoor things and went out on to the street. It was thawing. Sofia Petrovna came to a halt at a big puddle and had to concentrate all her attention on getting round it. Natasha caught up with her. Natasha already knew – Erna Semyonovna had told her.

"Natasha," Sofia Petrovna began when they came to the corner where they usually parted. "Natasha, do you believe that Zakharov is guilty of anything? No, it's such nonsense. Natasha, after all, we know . . ."

She could not find the words to express the certainty she felt. Zakharov, the Bolshevik, their director, whom they saw every day – how could he be a wrecker! It was an impossibility, rubbish, nonsense, as Fyodor Ivanovich used to say. Was it a misunderstanding? But he was such a prominent Party man, well known in the Smolny and in Moscow, that he couldn't be arrested by mistake. He was not like Kiparisov, for example.

Natasha remained silent.

"Let's go to your place and I'll explain everything to you immediately," Natasha said suddenly; she sounded unusually formal.

They went to Sofia Petrovna's, where they removed their

outdoor clothes in silence, and Natasha took from her tattered briefcase a carefully folded newspaper. She spread the paper out in front of Sofia Petrovna and pointed to a feature article on an inside page.

Sofia Petrovna put on her spectacles.

The article was about a certain Soviet citizen A., an honest Party member, who had been sent by the Soviet Government to Germany to learn how a recently invented chemical preparation was used. He carried out his work in Germany loyally, but it was not long before he was attracted by a certain C., an elegant young woman, allegedly a supporter of the Soviet Union. C. was a frequent visitor to A.'s apartment. Then one day citizen A. discovered that some very important political documents were missing from his desk. His landlady told him that C. had spent some time in his apartment in his absence. Citizen A. had the courage to break off relations with C. at once, but he was not brave enough to report the loss of the documents to his comrades. He returned to the USSR hoping by honest work as a Soviet engineer to make amends for the crime he had committed in the eyes of his Motherland. He worked away quietly for a whole year and had begun even to forget about his crime. But agents of the Gestapo managed to penetrate into the Soviet Union in disguise and started to blackmail him. Under pressure from them A. handed over secret plans of the factory where he worked. But the valiant secret police exposed the concealed agents of Fascism and the connections revealed by the investigation led to the unfortunate A.

"You see?" Natasha said in a whisper. "The connections revealed by the investigation. Our director is of course a good man and an honest Party member. But then so was citizen A. – they say that he was also at the beginning an honest Party man . . . Every honest Party man can be led astray by a pretty woman."

Natasha simply couldn't stand pretty women. She recognized only a sort of severe beauty which she found in nobody.

"They say our director did spend some time abroad," Natasha recalled. "He was also on an assignment. You remember, Maria Ivanovna the lift-girl said he brought his wife a blue knitted costume from Berlin."

Sofia Petrovna was very disturbed by the article, but she still didn't find it convincing. There was someone called A. and there was their own Zakharov. He was an experienced Party man who had himself made a speech about the trial. And under him the publishing house had always exceeded what was demanded by the plan.

"Natasha, after all, we know," Sofia Petrovna said in a tired voice.

"What do we know?" Natasha spoke up with some heat. "We know that he was director of our publishing house, and we don't really know another thing about him. Do you really know all about his life? Would you really be ready to vouch for him?"

To tell the truth Sofia Petrovna did not have the slightest idea what Comrade Zakharov was up to when he was not presiding over meetings at the publishers or leading his little girl around the fir-tree. Men – every single one of them – were terribly fond of pretty women. Any pert domestic servant was capable of hooking any man, even the most respectable. If Sofia Petrovna had not got rid of her servant Fani in good time there was no knowing how her flirting with Fyodor Ivanovich would have ended up.

"Let's have a cup of tea," Sofia Petrovna said.

Over the tea they recalled that Zakharov had a very military posture, with a straight back and broad shoulders. Had he not in his day been a White officer? He could well have been, judging by his age.

They just drank tea and nothing else. They were so exhausted that they hadn't the energy to go down to the shop for a loaf of bread or some cakes. "It will be very difficult in the office tomorrow," Sofia Petrovna was thinking. "It will be like having a corpse in the house. Say what you will but I'm sorry for the director." Then she remembered seeing the man on his knees at the desk through the half-open door of the director's office. Only then did she realize that the office was being searched.

Natasha was getting ready to leave. She folded up the newspaper carefully and put it away in her briefcase. Then before leaving she poured herself some hot water into a glass and warmed her big red hands against it. They had been frost-bitten when she was a child and were always cold.

Suddenly there was a ring at the door and then a second one. Sofia Petrovna went to open. Two rings – that was for her. Who could it be so late?

It was Alik Finkelstein standing in the doorway.

To see Alik alone without Kolya was unnatural.

"Where's Kolya?" Sofia Petrovna exclaimed, seizing Alik by the end of his scarf. "Is it typhoid?"

Without looking at her Alik slowly took off his galoshes.

"Shhh!" he said at last. "Let's go into your room."

He tiptoed down the corridor, looking rather funny with his short bow legs.

Sofia Petrovna followed him, quite beside herself.

"Now don't be alarmed for goodness' sake, Sofia Petrovna," he said when she had closed the door. "Just calm down: there's really no sense in being scared. It's nothing terrible. Ye – ye – yesterday . . . or when was it . . . ? be . . . be . . . before the last weekend . . . Kolya was arrested."

He sat down on the divan, unwound his scarf from his neck, threw it on the floor and burst into tears.

9

She felt she had to rush off somewhere straight away and clear up this monstrous misunderstanding. She would have to leave for Sverdlovsk that very minute and alert lawyers, the prosecutor's office, the judges and the investigators. Sofia Petrovna put on her overcoat, hat and shoes and took some money out of a box. She mustn't forget her identity card . . . She must be off to the station to buy a ticket.

But Alik, after wiping his face with his scarf, said that in his opinion there was absolutely no point in going to Sverdlovsk at the moment. As a person born and bred in Leningrad who had only recently gone to live in Sverdlovsk Kolya was most likely to be transferred to Leningrad. Would it not be better to delay the trip to Sverdlovsk for the time being? What if she missed him on the way? Sofia Petrovna took off her coat and threw her papers and money down on the table.

"The keys! Did you leave the keys there?" she cried out, advancing towards Alik. "Did you leave the keys with somebody?"

"Keys? What keys?" asked Alik, dumbfounded.

"My God, how stupid you are!" Sofia Petrovna exclaimed and then burst into tears, crying out loud. Natasha ran across and put her arm round her. "The key – of the room . . . in your, what do you call it . . . your hostel . . ."

They couldn't understand what she meant and simply looked at her blankly. What fools! Meanwhile Sofia Petrovna's throat had tightened and she couldn't speak. Natasha poured some water into a glass and handed it to her.

"Look – he . . . he," Sofia Petrovna said, pushing the glass aside – "He has already . . . probably . . . been released . . . they have realized that he is not . . . and they've let him out . . . he's gone home and found that you're not there and there's no key . . . We shall probably get a telegram from him any time now."

Still in her outdoor shoes Sofia Petrovna collapsed on to her bed. She went on crying, with her head sunk into a pillow, and cried and cried until the pillow was wet through. When finally she sat up her face was hurting and she could feel her heart beating violently in her breast.

Natasha and Alik were whispering to each other at the window.

"Listen," said Alik, giving her a kindly look over the top of his glasses. "Natalya Sergeyevna and I have worked out what to do. Get some sleep now and in the morning you will go quietly to the Prosecutor's office. Tomorrow at the publishers Natalya Sergeyevna will say that you are not well or that you had been affected in the night by fumes from the stove – something like that."

Alik left. Natasha wanted to stay the night, but Sofia Petrovna said she needed nothing at all. Natasha kissed her and departed. It looked as though she too had been crying.

Sofia Petrovna washed her face in cold water, undressed and went to bed. In the darkness the sparks from the tram-wires lit up the room like flashes of lightning. A square of white light thrown on to the wall and ceiling looked like a piece of paper folded in half. In the nurse's room Valya was still giggling away. Sofia Petrovna pictured to herself the situation when Kolya was brought under guard to the investigating officer, a handsome military man in a smart uniform and leather belt.

"You are Nikolai Fomich Lipatov?" the officer asks Kolya.

"I am Nikolai Fyodorovich Lipatov," Kolya replies with dignity.

The investigator gives the guard a severe reprimand and proceeds to make his apologies to Kolya.

"How on earth did I fail to recognize you? You're the young engineer whose picture I saw in *Pravda* recently. Please excuse us! The fact is that your namesake, Nikolai Fomich Lipatov, is a Trotskyist, a Fascist hireling and a wrecker . . ."

The whole night long Sofia Petrovna was expecting a telegram. When he went back to the hostel and found that Alik had gone to Leningrad Kolya would immediately send a telegram to reassure his mother. At six o'clock in the morning, when the trams came back to life, Sofia Petrovna fell asleep. She awoke again at the sharp ring of a bell which seemed to penetrate her heart. Was it a telegram? But the ring was not repeated.

Sofia Petrovna dressed, washed, forced herself to drink some tea and tidy the room. Then she went out on to the street – in a light mist. It was still thawing, but in the night a thin layer of ice had formed over the puddles.

After taking a few steps Sofia Petrovna came to a halt. Where exactly was she supposed to go?

Alik had told her to go to the Prosecutor's office. But Sofia Petrovna had no idea what the Prosecutor's office was, nor did she know where it was. And to enquire of passers-by about it seemed to her rather embarrassing. So she went, not to the Prosecutor's office, but to the prison because she happened to know that the prison was on Shpalernaya Street.

A guard armed with a rifle stood on duty at the iron gates. The little door next to the gates was closed. Sofia Petrovna gave the door a careful push with her hand and knee. There was nothing to say when the place opened.

The guard came across to her.

"They will start letting people in at nine o'clock," he said.

It was twenty minutes to eight. Sofia Petrovna decided not to return home. She walked up and down at the side of the prison, looking up and eyeing the metal grille.

Could it possibly be true that Kolya was there in that building behind bars?

'You can't walk here, citizen,'' said the guard.

Sofia Petrovna crossed to the other side of the road and walked on unsteadily without thinking where she was going. To her left she could see the vast snow-covered expanse of the frozen river Neva.

She turned left into a side street and came out on to the embankment.

It was getting light. With amazing unanimity the lamps on Liteynyi bridge went out. The Neva was piled high with dirty yellow snow. "They probably bring it here from all over the city,'' Sofia Petrovna thought to herself. Then she noticed a great crowd of women gathered in the street. Some were leaning on the embankment wall, others were moving slowly along the pavement and roadway. Sofia Petrovna was surprised to see how warmly dressed they all were: in heavy top coats wrapped round with scarves and nearly all of them in felt boots and galoshes. They stood around stamping their feet and blowing on their hands. "It looks as if they've been here a long time if they've got so cold,'' Sofia Petrovna speculated idly, "but it's not freezing, it's thawing again.'' All the women looked as though they had been waiting many long hours for a train at a country halt. Sofia Petrovna looked attentively at the building opposite which the women had gathered – a very ordinary building with nothing to indicate what went on inside it. So what were they all waiting for? The crowd included smartly dressed ladies and just ordinary women. For want of something better to do Sofia Petrovna walked a couple of times through the crowd. There was one woman with a babe in arms; she was holding the hand of another child wrapped tightly in a scarf. There was a man standing alone against the wall of the building. All their faces had a sort of greenish look. Perhaps it was the morning mist that made them look like that?

At one point a neat-looking little old lady with a stick came up to Sofia Petrovna. Her sealskin hat was pulled well down over her ears, and from beneath it her silver-grey hair peeped out, and her dark Jewish eyes.

"Do you need to go on the list?" the old lady asked in a friendly tone. "Go to the entrance of No. 28."

"What list?"

"Covering 'L' and 'M' . . . Oh, I'm sorry, citizen. You happen to be here and I thought you were also seeking information about someone who's been arrested."

"Yes, I am – about my son," Sofia Petrovna replied, somewhat bewildered.

Turning away from the old lady, who had given her an unpleasant surprise by the way she had guessed her purpose, Sofia Petrovna set off to find the entrance to No. 28. The thought that all those women had come there for the same reason as she was vaguely disturbing. But why were they standing there on the embankment and not outside the prison? Ah, yes, the guard would not allow them to gather near the prison.

No. 28 turned out to a rather run-down mansion almost next to the bridge. Sofia Petrovna went into the entrance hall, which was richly decorated but filthy, with a fireplace, a huge broken mirror and a marble figure of Eros without one of its wings. On the first step of the magnificent staircase there was a woman lying on a newspaper, her head resting on a rolled-up briefcase which was touched with the frost.

"You want to enter your name?" she asked, raising her head. Then she sat up and took a crumpled piece of paper and a pencil out of her briefcase.

"Well, I don't really know," Sofia Petrovna said, somewhat confused. "I have come along to speak to someone about my son who has been arrested by mistake in Sverdlovsk . . . You see, he just happened to have a namesake . . ."

"Please don't speak so loud," the woman interrupted her

crossly. She had an intelligent but tired face. "They confiscate the lists, and in any case . . . What's his surname?"

"Lipatov," Sofia Petrovna replied diffidently.

"Three hundred and forty-four," the woman said and wrote the number down. "Your number is 344. Now you must leave, please."

"Three four four," Sofia Petrovna repeated and went out again on to the embankment.

The crowd was even bigger now. "What number are you?" Sofia Petrovna kept being asked. "Well, you won't get called today," she was told by a woman in a peasant-style scarf. "We entered our names yesterday evening . . ." – "Where's the list?" – others asked in a whisper. By now it was fully light and a new day had begun.

Suddenly the whole crowd started to run and Sofia Petrovna ran with them. The child in the tightly tied scarf started to cry. He was bandy-legged and could hardly keep up with his mother. The crowd turned into Shpalernaya Street. Sofia Petrovna could see from afar that the little door next to the iron gates was now open. People were trying to squeeze their way in, like getting into a crowded tramcar. Sofia Petrovna forced her way in as well but was immediately brought to a halt – there was no way of going further. People were swarming all over the badly lit entrance hall and the little wooden staircase. The crowd swayed all together. They were all unwinding their scarves, unbuttoning their coats and trying to get somewhere: everyone was looking for the number preceding or following their own. More people kept pressing on from behind. Sofia Petrovna was carried along like a piece of wood in a stream. She undid her coat and wiped her forehead with her scarf. After she recovered her breath and had become accustomed to the dim light she also set about finding her next numbers – 343 and 345. Three forty-five was a man, and three forty-three was a very bent, ancient old woman. "Is your husband also a Latvian?" she asked, raising her lacklustre eyes to look at Sofia Petrovna. "No, why?" Sofia Petrovna replied. "Why Latvian? My husband died a long time ago, but he was a Russian."

"Tell me, please, do you have a ticket already?" Sofia Petrovna was asked by an old Jewess with silvery locks – the same one as she had talked to on the embankment.

Sofia Petrovna did not reply. She couldn't understand anything that was going on. The woman lying on the staircase; stupid questions about a Latvian and having a pass. What did you need a pass for? She had the impression that she was no longer in Leningrad but in some quite unfamiliar, strange city. It was strange to think that only half an hour's walk away was her office, the publishers and Natasha banging away at her typewriter.

Once they had found their neighbours in the list the people stood around quietly. Sofia Petrovna looked around: the little stairway led to a room in which there was also a crowd of people and, it appeared, there was another room beyond. She saw the woman with the briefcase, with woollen socks over her stockings and badly worn shoes – the one she had found lying on the stairway. People kept approaching, but she was no longer writing them down on the list – it was too late. It was awful to think that all those women were the mothers, wives and sisters of wreckers, terrorists and spies! And the man was a husband or a brother . . . To look at, they were the most ordinary people such as you would see in a tram or a shop. Only they all looked terribly tired and crushed. "I can well imagine what a misfortune it must be for a mother to learn that her son is a wrecker," Sofia Petrovna thought to herself.

From time to time a woman would make her way with difficulty through the crowd down the narrow creaking stairway. "Did you hand it in?" they would ask her down below. "Yes, I did," she would say and show them a piece of pink paper. But one of them, looking like a dairy-maid with a big milk-can in her hand, replied "He's been deported!" and bursting into tears, she put the can down and rested her head against the door-post. Her scarf slid down to reveal her reddish hair and little ear-rings. "Quiet!" came the warning from all sides. "He doesn't like noise – he'll close the door and that'll be that. Quiet!"

The dairy-maid tied her scarf back and went away, tears rolling down her cheeks.

Sofia Petrovna gathered from what was being said around her that the majority of the women had come to hand over money for their arrested husbands and sons, and some of them to enquire whether their husband or son was being held there. Sofia Petrovna's head was spinning because of the stuffy atmosphere and her own tiredness. She was very much afraid that the mysterious little window that they were all striving to reach would close before she managed to get to it. "If they are going to stay open only to two o'clock today, you and I are not going to make it," the man said. "Till two o'clock? Do we really have to stand around here till two o'clock?" Sofia Petrovna said to herself, appalled at the thought. "It's still only ten."

She closed her eyes in an effort to overcome her dizziness. There was a steady hum of brief, muttered exchanges.

"When did they take your man?"

"More than two months ago."

"It's only two weeks since mine went."

"Tell me, do you know anywhere else you can get information?"

"At the Prosecutor's office."

"Oh, but they don't tell you anything anywhere."

"Have you been to Chaikovsky Street, or to Herzen Street?"

"Herzen is for army people."

"When was yours arrested?"

"I have a daughter."

"They say they will accept underwear on Arsenalnaya Street."

"What are you, Latvians?"

"No, we're Poles."

"When did they come for your man?"

"Six months ago."

"What number have they got to now? Still in the twenties? My God, I do hope he won't shut down at two! Last time he slammed it shut on the very dot!"

Sofia Petrovna kept repeating to herself what she was going to ask: had Kolya been transferred to Leningrad? When would it be possible for her to see the judge or whoever it was – the investigator? Could it not be today? And would it not be possible to have a meeting with her son today?

Two hours later Sofia Petrovna, just behind the very old lady, had her foot on the first step of the wooden stairway. In three hours she reached the first room and after four hours she was in the second room. In five hours, at the end of a long winding queue she found herself again in the first room. Over other people's shoulders she got sight of the little square wooden window and beyond it the broad shoulders and big hands of a fat man. It was three o'clock. Sofia Petrovna calculated that there were still fifty-nine people ahead of her.

The women would call out their names and timidly pass some money through the window. The bandy-legged boy sobbed, licking away his tears with his tongue. "Well, now I shall be able to have a word with him," Sofia Petrovna thought impatiently. "I'll have him take me at once to the in-vestigator or the Prosecutor or whoever it is . . . How much is still lacking in our way of life! There's no air, they can't even ventilate the place. I ought to write a letter to the *Leningrad Pravda*."

And now, at last, there were only three people left ahead of Sofia Petrovna. She also prepared some money to hand in, just in case – there was no need for Kolya to go short while he was still under arrest. The old lady with a hunched back and trembling hands had handed thirty rubles in through the hatch and received in return a pink receipt, which she peered at with unseeing eyes. Sofia Petrovna quickly stepped into the old lady's place and found herself looking at an overweight young man with a white puffy face and narrow, sleepy eyes.

"I would like to know," Sofia Petrovna began, bending down so as to get a better view of the face of the man behind the hatch, "whether my son is here. The fact is, he's been arrested by mistake . . ."

"Surname?" the man cut her short.

"Lipatov. He was arrested by mistake, and it's some days now since I heard anything . . ."

"Be quiet, citizen," the man said, flicking through a card index. "Lipatov or Lepatov?"

"Lipatov. I would like to see the Prosecutor today or anyone else you may care to send me to . . ."

"What letters?"

Sofia Petrovna did not understand.

"What do they call him?"

"Ah – his initials. N. F."

"N or M?"

"N. Nikolai."

"Lipatov, Nikolai Fyodorovich," the man said, taking out a card. "He's here."

"I would like to know . . ."

"We do not give information. No more talk! Next!"

Sofia Petrovna hastily thrust thirty rubles through the hatch.

"He ain't allowed money," the man said, pushing the notes aside. "Next – Move along, woman – you're in the way."

"Move on!" somebody whispered to Sofia Petrovna from behind. "Otherwise he'll shut the hatch down."

By the time Sofia Petrovna made her way home it was going on for six o'clock, and Alik and Natasha were waiting for her. She collapsed into a chair and it was some minutes before she could find the strength to take off her own shoes and coat. Alik

61

and Natasha looked at her enquiringly. She told them that Kolya was in Leningrad, in the prison on Shpalernaya, but she just couldn't explain to them why she had not found out on what charge he had been arrested and when it might be possible to visit him.

10

Sofia Petrovna took two weeks' unpaid leave from the publishing house. So long as Kolya was in prison she could hardly put her mind to sorting out sheets of paper or dealing with Erna Semyonovna. In any case she would never have found the time to do her work on top of everything else: from morning to night and through the night she had to be standing in queues. She applied for leave to the lame Party organizer who, following Zakharov's arrest, had been appointed temporary director. He was now installed in the office that Zakharov had occupied, at the same big desk with three telephones, and he no longer wore a simple Russian shirt but a grey suit bought at the Leningrad Clothing Store and a collar and tie. But he still looked just as unprepossessing.

Sofia Petrovna said she needed some time off for domestic reasons. Without looking up at her Timofeyev took a long time to write out a certificate in red ink. He told Sofia Petrovna that this time she would be replaced by Erna Semyonovna and she was to hand her work over to Erna. "But why not Frolenko?" Sofia asked in a tone of surprise. "You know, Erna Semyonovna is almost illiterate and types a lot of mistakes . . ." Comrade Timofeyev made no reply and rose from his seat. Oh, what did it matter! Sofia Petrovna left the office. She was in a hurry to take up her place in the queue.

Sofia Petrovna's days and night were now no longer spent at home or at her work but in a new world, the world of the queue. She queued on the Neva embankment or she queued on

Chaikovsky Street – where there were benches to sit on – or she queued in the vast hall of the Great House, or on the staircase of the Prosecutor's office. She would go home to have something to eat or to sleep only when Natasha or Alik came to take her place in the queue. (Alik's boss had given him permission to go to Leningrad for no more than a week, but he kept putting off his departure for Sverdlovsk every day in the hope of travelling back along with Kolya.)

Sofia Petrovna learnt a great deal in the course of the two weeks – she learnt that it was best to take up her place in the queue at the end of the day, between eleven and twelve o'clock, and to return every two hours to confirm it, but that it was better not to leave the queue at all, so as not to lose her place. She learnt that it was essential to have a warm shawl with her and to wear felt boots, because, even when it was thawing, between three and six o'clock in the morning her feet could freeze with the cold and her whole body would start to shiver. She discovered that the lists drawn up by people in the queues were seized by secret police agents and that the person who put their names down was hauled off to the police station. She found out that you had to go to the Prosecutor's office on the first day of the week, but that you were not received there in alphabetical order . . . and that the families of men who were sentenced were deported from Leningrad, and that a "ticket" did not mean a trip to a holiday resort but a deportation order. She got to know that on Chaikovsky Street your questions were answered by a red-faced old man with a fluffy moustache, like a cat's, while at the Prosecutor's there was a girl with a permanent wave and a pointed nose. She discovered that among the enemies of the people who had been exposed there were a great many Latvians and Poles, which was why there were so many Latvian and Polish women in the queues. She learnt to guess immediately who among the people she saw on Chaikovsky Street was not just a passer-by but someone in the queue. Even in the tram she could tell by their eyes which of the women were on their way to the iron gates of the prison. She learnt how to find her way round all the doorways and backstairs of the houses on the embankment and had no difficulty in finding the woman with the list wherever she might be hiding.

Sofia Petrovna knew already as she left home after a brief sleep that on the streets and the stairways, in the corridors and the rooms, on Chaikovsky Street, on the embankment and in the Prosecutor's office, there would be women and more women and more women – old and young, some in shawls and some in hats, some with children at the breast, some with three-year-olds and some without children, some children crying for lack of sleep, and quiet, frightened women with little to say. It reminded her of how, in her childhood, after an excursion into the woods, she would shut her eyes and see nothing but berries and ever more berries – so now, when she closed her eyes, she saw nothing but faces, faces, faces . . .

There was only one thing she did not find out in the course of those two weeks – that was why Kolya had been arrested. By whom would he be tried and when? What was he accused of? And when would this ridiculous misunderstanding be finally cleared up and Kolya return home? At the information office on Chaikovsky Street the red-faced man with the fluffy moustache studied her identity card and enquired: "What is your son's name? You are his mother? Why did his wife not come? Not married? Lipatov, Nikolai? He is under interrogation." With that he tossed the identity card out of the hatch and before Sofia Petrovna had time to open her mouth the door of the hatch dropped with a bang and a bell rang to summon the next person. Sofia Petrovna had nothing she wanted to say to the door and, after hesitating a second or two, she moved away. At the Prosecutor's office the girl with the permanent wave and pointed nose poked her head out of the hatch and rattled off quickly: "Lipatov? Nikolai Fyodorovich? His papers have not yet reached the Prosecutor's office. Enquire again in a fortnight." On Shpa-lernaya the fat sleepy man pushed her money back as usual, saying: "He ain't allowed money." That was all she knew about Kolya – others *were* permitted to receive money, but for some reason he wasn't. Why? But she already realized that it was useless to put questions to the man at the hatch.

On the other hand she interrogated Alik greedily about what had happened and how Kolya had been taken away, and Alik dutifully told the story over and over again. They had been asleep when there had been a sudden knock on the door and the man in charge of the hostel had entered the room. He had been accompanied by the warden, a man in civilian clothes and one in army uniform.

"What time was it?" Sofia Petrovna asked.

"Oh, about half-past one," Alik replied and continued: "The warden switched the light on and the man in civvies asked: 'Which of you is Nikolai Lipatov?'"

"Was Kolya scared?" Sofia Petrovna enquired anxiously.

"Not in the slightest," Alik replied. "He put on his underwear and got into his suit and asked me to tell the factory that, through some misunderstanding, he had been arrested and that he might be off work for a few days. Yasha Roitman, one of our young Communists, should take over his duties."

"And did he really take nothing with him?" Sofia Petrovna asked, her hands clasped tightly together. Alik explained that Kolya refused to take a change of underwear or even a towel with him although it was there to take. "What's the point? I shall be back here tomorrow or the day after."

"I strongly advise you to take it," said the man in uniform.

But Kolya repeated that there was no point in doing so: he would be back the next day.

"That's what it means to have a clear conscience!" Sofia Petrovna said fondly. "But will they give him a towel there?"

Alik had waited loyally for Kolya a whole day, then two and

then three days. On the fourth day he decided to travel to Leningrad to find out what was going on. He told his boss a tale about his mother being at death's door, and the boss – a decent chap and a friend – let him go.

Sofia Petrovna continued putting carefully worded questions to Alik. Had Kolya quarrelled with his superiors? Had he offended someone? Had he been friendly with someone who had later turned out to be a wrecker? Or perhaps a woman had got him involved in some affair?

"Come on – what could a woman do to Kolya?" Alik replied with a touch of irritation in his voice. "Could anybody involve Nikolai in anything? Don't you know the sort of chap he is? Even his boss has said openly that he is a future world-class engineer."

Of course, of course, Kolya wasn't capable of doing anything stupid. Sofia Petrovna knew only too well what strength of character he had, what a head he had on his shoulders and how devoted he was to the Soviet regime and the Party. But, after all, nothing happens without some reason. Kolya was still a young man and had never lived on his own. Maybe he had caused someone to turn against him. One had to know how to get along with people. Sofia Petrovna cast an unfriendly glance at Alik: he hadn't taken good enough care of Kolya. If only Kolya had stayed in Leningrad under his mother's watchful eye nothing would have happened to him. She ought not to have let him go off to Sverdlovsk.

But in any case, Sofia Petrovna persuaded herself, nothing very bad could happen. Every hour, every minute she was expecting Kolya to turn up again. Whenever she went off to join the queue she would always leave the key to her own room in the corridor, on the little shelf in the usual place. She would even leave some soup ready for him in the oven. And on her return she would rush up the stairway without stopping for breath as she used to do in the hope of finding a letter from him. She saw herself entering her room and seeing Kolya there, home again, quite unable to understand where his mother had got to.

The previous night Sofia Petrovna had overheard one woman say to another: "Wait for him? He'll come back, will he? No one who fetches up in this place will return." Sofia Petrovna was about to butt in, but decided not to get involved. Innocent people were not kept in prison in the Soviet Union. Especially Soviet patriots like Kolya. The matter would be investigated and he would be released.

One evening, after persuading Sofia Petrovna to lie down at least for an hour, Alik put on his jacket, wrapped a scarf round his neck and took his leave. It was the 19th, and he was off to take his place in the queue on Shpalernaya Street. "I'll be there not later than two o'clock," Sofia Petrovna said in a faint voice from her bed.

"Sofia Petrovna, it's all right if you don't turn up till five," Alik replied cheerfully and left. But for some reason he came back and went up to Natasha who was sitting at the window holding her knitting.

"What do you really think, Natalya Sergeyevna," he asked, looking straight at her. "Do you think all those people there in that prison are just as guilty as Kolya is? All the mothers in the queue all look to me very much like Sofia Petrovna."

"I don't know," replied Natasha in her new laconic fashion.

Natasha had never been a very talkative person, but since Kolya had been arrested she had practically lost the power of speech. To every question she would reply simply "Yes" or "No" or "Don't know". It seemed as though, if you asked her what her name was, she would also reply "I don't know". She spent all her free time with Sofia Petrovna, preparing meals, washing the dishes, or standing in the queues – but almost never opening her mouth.

"Really, Alik," Sofia Petrovna said quietly. "How can you

make such a comparison! After all, Kolya has been arrested by mistake, while the others . . . Don't you read the papers?"

"Of course I read the papers," Alik replied and departed.

There had just been reports in the newspapers about the confessions made by people then being tried in the courts. As she had been standing in the queue the night before, Sofia Petrovna had read a whole page of a paper by peering over the shoulder of a man standing in front of her. Her feet were hurting and her heart was aching, but the paper was so interesting that, by stretching her neck, she could read it all. The accused spoke in great detail about murders, poisonings and explosions, and Sofia Petrovna was as appalled by what they said as was the Prosecutor. "And what do we call this?" the Prosecutor asked one of the accused with restrained indignation. "Treachery," the accused replied, completely mortified.

No, Sofia Petrovna had done right to keep away from her neighbours in the queues. She was sorry for them, of course, especially for the children, but an honest person had none the less to remember that all those women were the wives and mothers of poisoners, spies and murderers.

11

Two weeks passed. Alik went back to his factory in Sverdlovsk and Sofia Petrovna went back to work at the publishers, still having found out nothing about Kolya.

The women in the queue explained to her that Kolya's case was to arrive eventually at the Prosecutor's office, and when it did, she would be able to speak to the Prosecutor. He didn't receive people at a little window but at a desk, and you could tell him everything.

In the meantime there was nothing left for her to do but go to the office, count up the lines of typescript, smile, distribute the work and, to the clatter and bang of typewriters, think all the time about Kolya. Kolya was in prison, Kolya was in prison. Among thieves, spies and murderers. In a cell. Under lock and key.

When she tried to picture to herself what the prison looked like, and what Kolya looked like in it, what always came to mind was the picture of Princess Tarakanova – the grim wall and the young girl with tangled hair cowering back against it, the water on the floor, the rats . . . But of course it wasn't at all like that in a Soviet prison.

As he left, Alik advised her not to talk to anybody about Kolya's arrest. "I've no reason to be ashamed of Kolya!" Sofia Petrovna burst out angrily, but later she came to agree with Alik – other people didn't know Kolya and could imagine all sorts of things about him. Neither at work nor among her neighbours did she say anything to a soul, apart from Degtyarenko's wife, as she came across Sofia Petrovna on one occasion in the bathroom, crying. "Why are you crying? Maybe he'll come back yet," she said. "But I see you rushing around day and night, you look awful."

Five months had passed since the day of Kolya's arrest; winter made way for spring, and spring for a mercilessly hot June, but there was still no sign of Kolya. Sofia Petrovna was exhausted from the heat, the suspense, the standing in queues at night. Five months, three weeks and four days, and five days, and six days . . . five months and four weeks. But Kolya still did not appear, and he was still not allowed money. And then Sofia Petrovna began suddenly to have difficulties at work. They came one after the other.

The person responsible for causing the difficulties was Erna Semyonovna.

When Sofia Petrovna returned to work after her two weeks off Erna Semyonovna was left as her assistant – to check the typed manuscripts. Sofia Petrovna took the view that she would be of no assistance at all – semi-literate herself, how could she correct other people's mistakes? But it was useless to go against Timofeyev's orders. So Erna Semyonovna did the checking, and Sofia Petrovna remained silent.

Then one day the melancholy Comrade Timofeyev, with much rattling of his keys – he now always carried with him the keys of every single desk and room – stopped Sofia Petrovna in the corridor and asked her to send Frolenko to him after work. Sofia Petrovna sent Natasha to him in his office and stayed behind in the cloakroom waiting for her, wondering what on earth Timofeyev could want of Natasha.

Natasha soon appeared. Her features were bloodless, impassive; only her lips trembled a little. "I've been sacked," she said when they reached the street.

Sofia Petrovna stopped in her tracks.

"Erna Semyonovna showed the Party organizer the work I

did yesterday. You remember – it was a big article about the Red Army. In one place I had typed Rat Army instead of Red."

"But look here," Sofia Petrovna said, "that was just a simple typing slip. Where is it written that you should be sacked the next day? Everybody knows you are the best typist in the pool."

"He said I was being dismissed for lack of vigilance." Natasha walked on. The sun was shining straight into her eyes, but she didn't drop her gaze.

Sofia Petrovna took her home and gave her tea. No sign of Kolya. In the old days, when Kolya was living happily in Sverdlovsk, Sofia Petrovna never worried because he was not with her. Of course, she missed him. But now everything in her room screamed out at her that Kolya was not there. On the window-sill his gear-wheel still stood alone, losing its polish.

"I shall go to the publishers tomorrow, but that will be the last time," Natasha said as she left.

"Don't talk nonsense," Sofia Petrovna shouted after her. "It can't happen like that."

But it turned out that it could. Next day there was a notice on the wall in the corridor concerning the dismissal of N. Frolenko and E. Grigoryeva, former secretary of the director. The reason given for Frolenko's dismissal was "lack of political vigilance", and for the secretary's dismissal – "links with an exposed enemy of the people, the former director Zakharov".

Alongside the notice there was a big poster announcing that on that day at five o'clock in the afternoon there would take place a general meeting of all the employees. The agenda was: 1. Report by Comrade Timofeyev about the work of wreckers on the publishing front. 2. Other business. Attendance obligatory.

Natasha gathered up her little briefcase and left immediately after the bell, saying "goodbye" to everybody. "All the best," called the other typists in chorus. Only Erna Semyonovna did not react: she was combing her hair and admiring her reflection in the window-pane. Sofia Petrovna was very depressed and accompanied Natasha all the way to the cloakroom.

"Come round this evening," she said as they parted.

The chairman of the local committee was already gathering people together in the director's office. The lift-girl Maria Ivanovna was carrying in some chairs. Sofia Petrovna went into the room and sat down in the front row, feeling rather scared and quite alone. The lights were switched on and the big shutters closed. Then the other employees came in and took their seats. All their faces reflected an eager but fearful curiosity.

"What's the matter with you, comrades? Do I have to send you a special invitation?" the chairman called out in the editorial section.

Timofeyev stood at the desk and concentrated on sorting papers.

The chairman declared the meeting open. By an unenthusiastic show of hands she was elected chairman of the meeting. Comrade Timofeyev cleared his throat.

"We are gathered here this evening, comrades, because of a very important matter," he began. "We are here to take note of the presence in our publishing house of a criminal erosion of vigilance and jointly to consider how to eliminate the consequences of that situation." (He now spoke very confidently and smoothly and with hardly any stammering.) "For five whole years in this establishment of ours, under our very noses, if I may put it that way, there was at work in our community an enemy of the people who has now been exposed as a hardened criminal, a terrorist and a wrecker, the former director Zakharov. Zakharov has already been deprived of the possibility of doing further harm. But in his day he introduced into the business a whole string of his own admirers, his own suite, if I may use the word, which formed a closely knit group and did everything possible to help him in his dirty Trotskyist machinations. It is to the great shame of our community that Zakharov's suite has still not been liquidated to this day. I have here in front of me," he said unfolding some papers, "I have here facts on paper, facts providing you with documentary proof of their dirty counter-revolutionary work."

Timofeyev said no more and poured himself some water.

"What do these documents prove?" he started up again, wiping his face with the palm of his hand. "This document here proves irrefutably that in 1932, on the personal instructions of the director, without any reference to the local committee or the personnel department – I repeat, on personal instructions from the director – a certain N. Frolenko was given employment here."

Sofia Petrovna sat huddled up on her chair, feeling as though he was talking about her.

"And who is this Frolenko? She is the daughter of a colonel, the owner of what was known in the old days as an estate. What, it may be asked, was this lady Frolenko, daughter of someone alien to our society, doing in our Soviet publishing house, employed by the gangster Zakharov? The answer is to be found in another document. Under the protecting wing of Zakharov citizen Frolenko found it possible to slander our beloved Workers' and Peasants' Red Army, to organize counter-revolutionary attacks: she called the Red Army the Rat Army."

Sofia Petrovna's mouth was quite dry.

"And what about the former secretary Grigoryeva? She was the director's faithful assistant in whom he could have absolute confidence in all his work, if I can use such a word. How could it come about that a wrecker and his hanger-on were able for five long years so blatantly to deceive a Soviet community? It can be explained, comrades, by one thing alone – the criminal erosion of political vigilance."

Comrade Timofeyev sat down and took a drink of water. Sofia Petrovna eyed the water thirstily – her mouth and throat were so very dry. The chairman rang the bell, although everybody remained silent and no one moved.

"Does anyone wish to speak?" she asked.

Silence.

"Comrades – does anyone wish to take the floor?" the chairman asked again.

Silence.

"Is there really nobody who wishes to say a few words on such a burning issue?"

Silence. Then suddenly there was a loud voice coming from the direction of the door. Everybody looked round.

It was the lift-girl, Maria Ivanovna, who had so far never spoken at any meeting at all. There were in fact very few people in the publishers who had ever heard her voice.

"Please, please – come up here, Comrade Ivanovna!"

The lift-girl clumped up to the desk.

"I would also like to say my proletarian word about this. What's been said about the secretary, comrades, is true. She used to get into the lift in her galoshes and mess up the floor and I had to clean up after her. She made the mess and I cleaned it up. I would take her up to the top, and next thing she wants the lift to go down in. She'd go up a hundred times, but always down in the lift as well. And I couldn't very well refuse when she was always right next to the director. Wherever he went she went too. If he got in the lift, in she would go after him. If he went by car there she was, sitting next to him. It's true – they worked hand in glove. Only I would like to say to Comrade Timofeyev, in our language, simply, like a worker: how many times did I report this to him? 'Get rid of the fancy lady,' I said, but he didn't give a damn! – paid no attention at all, dismissed me with a wave of his hand. Do you think, Comrade Timofeyev, that a lift-girl is just a little person who doesn't understand? You're wrong! These are not the old days; under the Soviet regime there are no little people – we are all big people."

"Quite right, Comrade Ivanovna, quite right," said Anna Grigoryevna. "Who else would like to speak, comrades?"

Silence.

"May I?" Sofia Petrovna enquired quietly. She stood up, but sat down again. "I would like to say just a few words about Frolenko. Of course it is terrible, quite awful, what she typed . . . but, after all, everybody makes mistakes at work, don't they? She wrote 'Rat' instead of 'Red' simply because, as every typist knows, the letters are placed close together on the typewriter. It was a simple mistake. Frolenko was a highly qualified employee and very diligent. It was just an accident."

Sofia Petrovna said no more.

"Do you wish to reply?" the chairman asked Timofeyev.

"Here are the documents," Timofeyev replied from behind the desk and tapped on the papers with his knuckles. "You can't fly in the face of the documents, Comrade Lipatova. A hostile attack motivated by class feelings on the part of citizen Frolenko is there for all to see."

"Anybody else wish to speak? I declare the meeting over."

People quickly dispersed, eager to get home. In the cloakroom people were chatting – the No. 5 tram was not very frequent, they said, and some beautiful knickers were on sale at the Passage in the children's department. The accountant was urging Erna Semyonovna to go sailing with him.

"You and your boat!" she said, pouting her lips at the mirror as if to kiss it. "I wouldn't mind going to the cinema."

But not a word about the meeting or about the wreckers.

Sofia Petrovna hurried home, scarcely looking where she was going. She had the idea that once she was in her own room and had shut the door her head would stop aching, everything would stop, and she would feel all right. Now her temples were throbbing. Why did she have such a headache? People had not been smoking at the meeting. Poor Natasha! Nothing went right for her in life. An excellent typist and then all of a sudden . . .

In her room on Kolya's desk there was a note waiting for her. "Dear Sofia Petrovna! I am back again. Yasha Roitman has reported me to the young Communist organization for being connected with Nikolai. I have been expelled from the organization because I refused to dissociate myself from Nikolai, and I have been sacked. It is very hard to be expelled from the ranks. I will drop in tomorrow. Yours, Aleksandr Finkelstein."

Sofia Petrovna turned the note over and over. My God, she thought, so many unpleasant things at once! Kolya, then Natasha, and now Alik. But Alik probably had only himself to blame: he may have said too much at some meeting. He had become so sharp-tongued. On the day of his departure, when she had asked him again very cautiously whether Kolya had perhaps got mixed up with bad people, he had flared up, pressed himself back against the wall and shouted at her: "Do you realize what it is you're asking? Kolya is not guilty of anything at all – do you have any doubts?" Of course he was not guilty of anything – silly to talk about it – but had Kolya provided any grounds on which to accuse him? Now, at the meeting, Alik had probably provoked the people in charge. Of course, he had to stand up for Kolya, but with a little more caution, with greater tact and restraint . . .

Sofia Petrovna had a headache. For her the meeting seemed to be still going on. Timofeyev's voice was still ringing in her ears. She felt a tightness in her chest and it seemed to her as though Timofeyev's voice was the cause of it. Should she lie down? No, she decided to take a bath.

There had been something in Timofeyev's words that seemed to have taken all the life out of her body. She had the idea that, if she had a bath, the feeling would go away. She fetched some wood from the store and lit the boiler. In the old days it was always Kolya who brought her wood in, then it had been Alik, and after his second departure for Sverdlovsk Natasha had done

77

it. Oh dear, that young Alik! He was a good lad, of course, and quite devoted to Kolya – but so outspoken. He had no business being so quick-tempered. Was it not on account of his sharp tongue that Kolya was in prison? Once, as they were standing in the queue on Shpalernaya and she told Alik that they had again refused to take the money for Kolya, he had shouted out loud: "Blasted bureaucrats!" He might behave in the same way in the factory in Sverdlovsk.

Sofia Petrovna ran her bath, undressed and sat in the tub – the ample white tub that Fyodor Ivanovich had bought. She didn't want to wash herself. She just lay motionless, her eyes closed. What would it be like for her now in the office without Natasha? And it was all because of that Erna Semyonovna! There were such envious, malicious people in the world. Well, never mind, Natasha would find another job, somewhere not too far away and they would see each other quite often. If only Kolya would come back soon.

She lay there staring at her hands which looked so different in the water. Could the director's secretary really have been a wrecker? It was better not to think about it. What a difficult day it had been. She was still depressed by the thought of the meeting. She lay there, warm and peaceful, with her eyes closed.

Someone turned off the primus stove in the kitchen and there was the sound of voices and the clatter of dishes. The nurse was, as usual, making caustic remarks.

"I am not yet out of my mind and I still keep my eyes open," she declared ponderously. "Two days ago I personally bought three litres of paraffin. Now there's only a drop in the bottom. For some time now it has been impossible to leave anything in the kitchen."

"Who's going to take your paraffin?" Degtyarenko's wife said in her deep voice. By her voice she would seem to have been bending down, wiping the floor or lighting the stove. "People have got enough paraffin of their own. Do you think it's me?"

"I'm not talking about you. There are other people living in the flat besides you. If there is one member of a family already in prison you can expect anything from the rest. People aren't sent to prison for doing good."

Sofia Petrovna froze.

"What if her son *is* in prison," said Degtyarenko's wife. "He'll go down for a bit and then he'll be released. He's not a pickpocket or a thief. He's a well educated young man. They are sending all sorts of people to prison these days. My husband says a lot of decent people are being arrested. And they wrote about him in the paper. He was a famous shock-worker."

"Some shock-worker. He was just putting it on." That was Valya's voice.

"So he was an innocent lamb, was he?" the nurse pursued. "No, I'm sorry, but in our country people are not sent to prison for nothing. Just forget it. *I* am not in prison. Why not? Because I'm an honest woman and entirely Soviet."

Sofia Petrovna felt cold in the bath. Shivering all over she wiped herself dry, put on a dressing-gown and tiptoed to her room. She lay beneath the blanket and put a pillow on her feet. But she continued to shiver. She lay there, still shaking, and stared straight ahead into the darkness.

During the night, around two o'clock, when everybody was asleep, she slipped an overcoat over her nightdress and went to the kitchen. She took her oil-stove, her primus and her saucepans and brought them back to her room.

It was not until nearly morning that she fell asleep.

12

Next day Alik was waiting for her at the entrance to the publishers. It appeared that, without saying anything to her, so as not to cause her unnecessary worry, he and Natasha had from early morning been standing in the queue for the Prosecutor's office. They had done it for six hours, taking it in turns, and half an hour ago the young lady at the little window had told them that the case of Nikolai Lipatov was now with the Prosecutor Tsvetkov. They then took a place for Sofia Petrovna in the queue for Prosecutor Tsvetkov. For room No. 7.

Alik tried to persuade Sofia Petrovna to go home first and have something to eat, but she was afraid of losing her place in the queue and set out quickly, as fast as she could go. She was going to rescue Kolya. She strode along, out of breath, and as she went she was thinking up the speech she was going to make. She would tell the Prosecutor about the way Kolya joined the young Communists as a boy, almost against his mother's wishes; what a good student he had been at school and college; how much his work was appreciated at the factory and how he had been praised in *Pravda*. He was a remarkable engineer, an honest young Comunist and a caring son. Could anyone really suspect such a person of being involved in wrecking or counter-revolution? What nonsense, what a fantastic suggestion! She, his old mother, would bear witness in court that it was not true.

Alik opened the heavy door and she went in.

Sofia Petrovna had recently seen a great many queues, but

she had never seen one like this. People were standing, sitting and lying right up the stairway, on all the landings and all the window-sills of a huge five-storey staircase. It was impossible to go up it without stepping on somebody's arm or stomach. In the corridor, next to a little window and the door of room No. 7 people were standing packed close together as if they were in a tram. They were the lucky ones who had already made their way up the whole stairway. Natasha was hunched up by the wall beneath a large poster which said "Raise higher the banner of the revolutionary rule of law!" Sofia Petrovna and Alik came to a halt and both tried to regain their breath. Alik took off his steamed-up glasses and wiped them with his fingers.

"So I'm off," Natasha said at once. "You are next to that lady over there."

Sofia Petrovna had wanted to tell Natasha about the meeting on the previous day and about what she had said in her defence, but Natasha's back was already disappearing in the distance.

"Natalya Sergeyevna's in a real fix," said Alik pointing his chin in her direction. "They won't take her on anywhere. It's the same with me."

It appeared that Natasha had already had time to apply to several establishments that needed typists, but no one would take her on once they had checked with her previous place of employment. Alik had gone straight from the railway station to apply for work at a design office, but as soon as they knew he had been expelled from the young Communist organization they wouldn't even talk to him.

"I know we are marked people. What scoundrels they are! Where have all these bastards suddenly sprung from?" Alik said.

"Alik!" said Sofia Petrovna reproachfully. "How can you? It's for that quick tongue of yours that they expelled you from the young Communists."

"No, not for that, Sofia Petrovna," Alik replied, his lips

trembling slightly. "But because I would not dissociate myself from Nikolai."

"No, Alik," Sofia Petrovna said softly, laying her hand on his sleeve. "You are still very young – I assure you you are wrong. Everything depends on having a little tact. Yesterday, for example, at the meeting I defended Natalya Sergeyevna. And what happened? Nothing happened to me. Believe me, the affair with Kolya has caused me great pain. I am his mother. But I understand that it's a temporary misunderstanding, a case of somebody overstepping the mark, a weakness in the system . . . we just have to be patient. But you shout out straightaway: 'rogues and scoundrels!' Remember, Kolya always said there is still a great deal in our country that is imperfect and bureaucratic."

Alik said nothing. His face was set in an expression of stubborn determination. He was unshaven, his cheeks were sunken and there were dark patches beneath his eyes. And the way he looked over the top of his glasses had changed: his look was a grim scowl.

"I have already made my application to the district committee. If they don't restore me to membership I shall go to Moscow, right to the Central Committee of the young Communists' League."

"Poor lad!" Sofia Petrovna thought. "He's going to find it difficult so long as he has no job. His aunt is probably reproaching him already." Leaning closer to Alik, Sofia Petrovna whispered: "As soon as they release Kolya you'll be taken back." She smiled fondly at him. But Alik did not smile back.

It was still a long way to the Prosecutor's door. Sofia Petrovna counted forty people ahead of her. They went in two at a time, because in room No. 7 there were two Prosecutors working, and still the queue moved very slowly. Sofia Petrovna looked round at all the faces: she had the impression that she had seen most of the women before – on Shpalernaya Street or on

Chaikovsky Street, or there at the Prosecutor's office by the little window. Perhaps they were the same people, perhaps not. There was something similar in the expressions of all women standing in queues at prison gates: a mixture of fatigue, submission and a sort of reticence. Many of them were holding pieces of white paper in their hands, and Sofia Petrovna already knew that they were the "tickets" for deportation. In her queue there were three questions being continually repeated: "Where are you going to?" – "When are you going?" – "Has your property yet been confiscated?"

Sofia Petrovna leaned against the wall and closed her eyes for a minute. What a heartless, malicious and stupid woman the accountant's wife was! To imagine that Kolya could be a wrecker! After all, she had known him since childhood. Sofia Petrovna vowed never to cross the threshold of the kitchen again, at least until such time as the woman apologized. Just imagine how ashamed she would be when Kolya returned. Sofia Petrovna would tell Kolya everything – about his wonderful friends, Natasha and Alik (without whom she would never have been able to cope with the queues) and with that snake in the grass, the accountant's wife. Kolya must know the sort of scoundrels you came across in life.

When she opened her eyes Sofia Petrovna noticed a little girl squatting down by the wall. She was in a winter coat buttoned up to the neck. "Why have we got into the habit of always wrapping children up even in summer?" Sofia Petrovna thought. Then suddenly, when she looked more closely, she recognized the little girl – it was the daughter of Zakharov, the director. She was wriggling with her back against the wall and whining, obviously suffering from the heat. And the tall, well-built woman in a light-coloured suit, behind whom Sofia Petrovna and Alik had been standing for an hour already, was the director's wife. Of course it was.

"Do you still have your little tin whistle," Sofia Petrovna

asked the girl in a motherly way. "Or have you already lost the little tassel? Do you remember me? At the fir-tree? Here, let me open up your coat at the neck for you."

The little girl remained silent, eyeing Sofia Petrovna with wondering eyes and holding on to her mother's hand.

"What's the matter with you? Answer the lady!" said the director's wife.

"I knew your husband," Sofia Petrovna said, turning to her. "I work at the publishing house."

"Oh!" said the director's wife, grimacing as though in pain. She was wearing lipstick, but it spread beyond the edges of her lips. She was unquestionably a good-looking woman, but she no longer looked to Sofia Petrovna as young and smartly dressed as she had done six months previously when she had dropped in to the publishers to see her husband and had replied in a friendly way to the greetings from employees in the corridor.

"What is the situation with you husband?" Sofia Petrovna enquired.

"Ten years in a remote camp."

("That means he was guilty after all. I would never have thought it. Such a pleasant person," said Sofia Petrovna to herself.)

"And I'm being sent with her to Kazakhstan – to some village or other . . . I leave tomorrow. I shall die of hunger there without work."

She spoke in a loud, aggressive voice, and everyone turned to look at her.

"And where has your husband been sent?" Sofia Petrovna asked, so as to change the subject.

"How should I know where he's gone? Do you think they tell you?"

"But how will you later . . . after the ten years . . . when he is released . . . find each other? You won't know his address nor he yours."

"Do you really think," said the director's wife, "that a single one of these people" – she indicated with her hand the crowd of women with their "tickets" – "knows where her husband is? The husband has already been shipped off, or will be tomorrow or even today. The wife is also departing for some God-forsaken place and hasn't the foggiest idea how she will later find her husband. How can I hope to find out? Nobody knows, and I don't know."

"You have to be persistent," Sofia Petrovna replied quietly. "If they won't tell you here, you must write to Moscow. Or go to Moscow. Otherwise you will lose contact with each other."

The director's wife looked her up and down. "Well, who have you got? A husband? A son?" she asked with such vehemence that Sofia Petrovna moved instinctively closer to Alik.

"So, when they ship your son off then it will be up to you to display persistence and to find out his address."

"My son will not be shipped off," Sofia Petrovna said in an apologetic tone. "The fact is, he is not guilty. He was arrested by mistake."

'Ha – ha – ha!" The director's wife burst into a loud guffaw. "Ha – ha – ha! By mistake!" And suddenly tears welled up in her eyes. "Don't you realize that everyone is here by mistake. . ? Do stand still!" she shouted at her little girl and bent over her to conceal her tears.

There were now five people between Sofia Petrovna and the door. Sofia Petrovna repeated to herself again the words she would say to the Prosecutor. She felt sorry for the director's wife in a condescending way. Very fine husbands, she must say. They caused a lot of trouble and left their wives to suffer on their account. She was now off to Kazakhstan with her child, and those queues – you could hardly help ending up a tangle of nerves.

"You know, I think I'll come with you," said Alik suddenly. "As a colleague and a friend. I'll tell the comrade Prosecutor that we have in Nikolai a person of crystal-clear character, an unyielding Bolshevik. I will tell him about the introduction to our factory of the Fellows gear-cutter, for which we are indebted exclusively to Nikolai's inventiveness."

But Sofia Petrovna did not want Alik to come in with her to the Prosecutor. She feared the sharpness of his tongue; he would be too outspoken and put his foot in it. No, it was better for her to go alone. She assured Alik that the Prosecutor did not admit people who were not related.

At last her turn came. The director's wife opened the door and entered. Her heart sinking, Sofia Petrovna followed her in.

At two opposite walls of a large, empty and badly lit room stood two desks with two tattered armchairs in front of them. At the desk to the right sat a fat man with a pale face and blue eyes. At the table to the left sat a hunchback. The director's wife and her daughter went across to the pale-faced man. Sofia Petrovna went to the hunchback. She had already heard long ago in the queues that Prosecutor Tsvetkov was a hunchback.

Tsvetkov was talking on the telephone. Sofia Petrovna sank into the armchair.

Tsvetkov was a small thin man wearing a blue, rather dirty suit. His little head was pointed, the hump on his back rounded. His long fingers and the back of his hands were covered with black hair. He didn't hold the telephone receiver in the normal, human way but the way monkeys do. Altogether he looked to Sofia Petrovna so like a monkey that the thought came involuntarily to her mind – that if he should want to scratch behind his ear he would probably do it with his foot.

"Fyodorov?" Tsvetkov shouted hoarsely down the receiver. "This is Tsvetkov – hello. Tell Panteleyev that I've pushed everything through already. Let him send them here. What? I said let him send them."

At the other table the fat man with bright doll-like eyes and small, chubby woman's hands was chatting politely with the director's wife.

"I would like to be transferred from the village to some town," she said, standing at the desk and holding her child's hand. "In a village there will be no work for me. I shall have no means of supporting my child and my mother. I am a shorthand-typist by profession and there will be no work for me in a village. I beg you not to send me to a village but to a town, even if it has to be in – what do you call it? – Kazakhstan."

"Please be seated, citizen," the pale-faced man said kindly.

"What are you after?" Tsvetkov asked Sofia Petrovna, having replaced the telephone and darting her a brief glance with his little black eyes.

"I have come about my son. His name is Lipatov. He was arrested through a misunderstanding, a mistake. I was told that you are dealing with his case."

"Lipatov?" Tsvetkov repeated, trying to recall. "Ten years in remote camps." He picked up the telephone again. "Section A? 244–16."

"What's that? You mean to say he's already been sentenced?" Sofia Petrovna exclaimed.

"244–16? Call Morozova to the phone."

Sofia Petrovna remained silent, holding her hand to her heart. She could feel it beating very slowly and she could hear it in her ears and at her temples. Sofia Petrovna decided to wait until Tsvetkov stopped talking on the telephone. The sight of his long hairy hands, his hump covered in dandruff, and his yellow unshaven face struck fear into her. She must be patient. She went on listening to the beating of her heart, at her temples and in her ears. Meanwhile, at the opposite table the pale-faced Prosecutor was saying to the director's wife: "There's no point in your getting so upset, citizen. Please sit down. As representative of the law I am obliged to remind you that the great Stalin Constitution guarantees to everybody without distinction the right to work. In view of the fact that no one has deprived you of any civil rights your right to work is assured, wherever you may be living."

Without more ado the director's wife stood up and made for the door. The little girl ran after her in little uneven steps.

"You still here? What do you want?" Tsvetkov demanded roughly when he had put the phone down.

"I would like to know what my son could be guilty of," Sofia Petrovna asked, calling on all her resources to prevent her voice from trembling. "He was always an exemplary young Communist and an honest citizen . . ."

"Your son has confessed to his crimes. The investigating department has his signature. He is a terrorist and he took part in an act of terrorism. Do you understand?"

Tsvetkov was opening and shutting the drawers of his desk. He would open a drawer and then bang it shut. The drawers were empty.

Sofia Petrovna racked her brain in an effort to recall what else she had meant to say. But her mind was a blank. And in any case, in that room, faced with such a man, all words were meaningless. She stood up and made her way to the door.

"How can I find out now where he is?" she asked at the door.

"That has nothing to do with me."

The faithful Alik was waiting for her in the corridor. Without saying anything they squeezed their way through the crowd, along the corridor and down the staircase. They went silently out on to the street. There the trams were rattling along, the sun was shining and the pavement was crowded with people. It was still very early on an airless summer's day.

"What happened, Sofia Petrovna, tell me," Alik asked anxiously.

"He's been sentenced. To remote camps. For ten years."

"You're joking!" Alik exclaimed. "What for?"

"For taking part in an act of terrorism."

"Kolya – an act of terrorism? They must be mad!"

"The Prosecutor says that he confessed. They have got his signature."

Tears streamed down Sofia Petrovna's cheeks. She halted by the wall and held on to a water-pipe.

"Kolya Lipatov a terrorist!" Alik said, choking with rage. "Bastards – what bastards they are! That's rich! You know, Sofia Petrovna, I am beginning to think that this is all some kind of colossal sabotage operation. The wreckers have penetrated the secret police and are running the whole show. They are themselves the enemies of the people."

"Yes, but Kolya has confessed, Alik, he has confessed, Alik, you must understand," Sofia Petrovna sobbed.

Alik took Sofia Petrovna firmly by the arm and led her home. At the door of her apartment, while she was looking for her key in her handbag he told her once again: "Kolya had nothing to confess: surely you have no doubts on that score? I no longer understand anything, anything at all. There's one thing I would now like to do – to talk to Comrade Stalin face to face. Let him explain to me what he thinks is going on."

13

The whole night through Sofia Petrovna lay with open eyes. She had lost count of how many nights had now passed since Kolya's arrest – it was just endless, bottomless night. She now recognized every sound instinctively – the shuffling of feet beneath her window in summer, shouts coming from the bar nearby, the screech of trams fading into the distance, then the brief period of silence and darkness before the pale dawn crept once again to the window and another day began, another day without Kolya. Where was Kolya now, what had he to sleep on, what was he thinking about, where was he, with whom was he? Sofia Petrovna did not doubt for a single moment that he was innocent. An act of terrorism? – madness, as Alik had said. He must simply have come up against an investigator who was too keen on his job and had tripped him up. Kolya didn't know how to defend himself, he was still so young. Towards morning, as it became light again, Sofia Petrovna at last remembered the word she had been searching for all night – alibi. She had read about it somewhere. He had simply not been able to produce an alibi.

She felt rather better for an hour or two back at work. The sun shone brightly, its rays lighting up the dust floating in the air, and the typewriters rattled away busily, and in their break the typists rushed down to the street and came back licking ice-creams. Everything quite normal . . . Ten years! In the light of day with the sun shining it became quite clear that the whole affair was just nonsense. She was not going to see Kolya for ten years! But why? What nonsense was this? It just couldn't be. One fine day – and quite soon – everything would be back as it was before: Kolya would be home, arguing with Alik about motor-cars and locomotives and working on his designs, only this time there would be no question of her letting him go to Sverdlovsk. He could find himself a job in Leningrad.

During her lunch-break she went out into the corridor to stretch her legs: she was afraid she would drop off to sleep if she remained sitting. There was a fresh wall newspaper hanging in the corridor, and a crowd of employees reading it. Sofia Petrovna joined them. It was a big, well produced number with the initial capitals in red and portraits of Lenin and Stalin beside the title of the paper in bright red – *Our Path*. Sofia Petrovna started to read the text.

"How could it happen that for five long years wreckers were able without any interference to do their dirty work under the very noses of the Soviet public?" Sofia Petrovna read.

That was Timofeyev's leading article. In the next column was the beginning of an article by the chairman of the local committee, Anna Grigoryevna, accusing Timofeyev in the bitterest terms of not being more self-critical in his speech at the meeting. If the community had failed to notice the wrecking activity going on it was primarily the responsibility of Comrade Timofeyev, the former Party organizer. Especially since, as had become apparent, the Party organizer had been warned in good time by Comrade Ivanovna who, with her proletarian instinct, had long ago seen through the secretary. Sofia Petrovna looked across to the next column. Before she realized what she was reading she grew hot and cold all over. The article was about herself, Sofia Petrovna, about what she had said in defence of Natasha. The author of the article, hiding behind the pseudonym X., had written:

"Something really scandalous took place at the meeting, which was, in our opinion, too lightly dealt with. Comrade

91

Lipatova spoke up like a real defence lawyer. And who did she find it necessary to defend? Frolenko, the colonel's daughter who had permitted herself to make a crude anti-Soviet attack on our beloved Workers' and Peasants' Red Army. We know that Comrade Lipatova has always protected Frolenko, providing her with overtime work, gone with her to the cinema and so on. Now, when the publishing house is faced with the need for honest employees and Party and non-Party Bolsheviks to strain every sinew so as to liquidate with all speed the consequences of the 'management' by Gerasimov, Zakharov and Co., is it permissible at such a crucial moment for people such as she to be among the employees of our firm? Raise high the banner of Bolshevik vigilance, as we are taught by the genius and leader of the peoples, Comrade Stalin. We will root out all wreckers, hidden and exposed, and all those who have indicated their sympathy for them!"

The bell rang to mark the end of the lunch-break. Sofia Petrovna went to her office. How had she failed to notice earlier that they had been giving her strange looks from the start of the day?

When she returned home she sank her head in her pillow – her last refuge – and soon fell asleep. She slept for a long time, dreaming of Kolya. He was wearing a fluffy grey sweater and tying his skates on. Then with a deep bow he skated along the corridor of the publishers' office. When she awoke it was already twilight outside the window and the light was on in the room. Natasha was sewing at the table. She had obviously been there for some time.

"Come and sit over here, nearer to me," Sofia Petrovna said in a weak voice, moistening her lips which had a bad taste after daytime sleep.

Natasha obediently brought her chair over to the bedside and sat down.

"You know Kolya has been sentenced, to ten years. Alik probably told you?"

Natasha nodded.

"Oh, have you heard?" Sofia Petrovna remembered. "They have written about me in the wall newspaper, saying I defend wreckers and have no place . . ."

"Alik's been arrested – last night," Natasha said.

14

When Sofia Petrovna was unable to sleep at night every hour and every minute was exactly the same for her. The light hurt her eyes, her legs were painful and her heart ached. But if she did manage to get to sleep then there was no doubt that the most difficult moment came just after she woke. When she opened her eyes and saw the window, the end of the bed and her dress lying on the chair, she thought of nothing in that first moment apart from those objects. She would recognize them – the window, the chair and the dress. But the very next moment she felt a sense of alarm, like a real pain, and through the mist of that pain she would recall everything at once – Kolya sentenced to ten years, Natasha thrown out, Alik arrested, and she herself accused of being in league with the wreckers. And on top of that, the story of the paraffin.

At work she no longer talked to anybody. Even the material that was brought to her for copying she handed over to the typists without a word. And nobody spoke to her. As she sat at her desk in the typing pool she studied the faces of the typists, trying to guess which one of them had written the article about her. The most likely one was Erna Semyonovna. But was she really capable of being so articulate? And when had she ever seen her with Natasha at the cinema? They had never seen her.

On one occasion when she was listlessly strolling along the corridor she nearly bumped into Natasha, who was behaving like a sleep-walker, taking tentative steps as if in the dark.

"Natasha, what are you doing here?" Sofia Petrovna asked in alarm.

"I have read the article. Don't talk to me – they will see us," Natasha replied.

That evening she visited Sofia Petrovna. She now seemed to be strangely excited and kept up a continuous chatter, skipping from one subject to the next. Sofia Petrovna had never known Natasha so talkative. Moreover, she was not embroidering or sewing.

"What do you think – is Kolya still here in this city or is he already a long way away?" she asked suddenly.

"I don't know, Natasha," Sofia Petrovna replied with a sigh. "At Shpalernaya his number comes up on the 20th, and today we're only the 10th."

"No, I don't mean that. What do you *feel*?" Natasha waved her hand in the air. "Is he still here, near to us, or is he far away? It seems to me he's far away. Yesterday I suddenly felt it – now he's a long way away. He's no longer here . . . Do you know, Sofia Petrovna, the lift-girl refused to take me up in the lift. 'I'm not obliged to take everybody who happens to come along' . . . Yes, Sofia Petrovna, you must leave the publishing house immediately, tomorrow. Promise me that you will leave. Promise me, please. Tomorrow – all right?"

Natasha was kneeling on the divan on which Sofia Petrovna was sitting, and she clasped her hands pleadingly towards her. Then she sat down at the table, took up a pen and wrote Sofia Petrovna's letter of resignation for her. She assured Sofia Petrovna that it was essential for her to leave at her own wish, otherwise she would surely be dismissed for being connected with wreckers – "with me, that is," added Natasha with a smile on her pale lips – and then she wouldn't get another job anywhere. Sofia Petrovna signed the letter. She had anyway been thinking of leaving. It had become rather frightening at the publishers. The very sight of the limping Timofeyev with his bunch of keys in his hand sent a shiver up her spine.

"But I shan't be able to work in Leningrad in any case," she said sadly. "I shall be deported at all events. The wives and mothers are all being deported."

"What do you think?" Natasha asked, taking a book from the shelf and straightaway replacing it. "How can you explain the fact that Kolya confessed? I realize that a person can be worn down and become confused, but only over relatively trivial matters. How is it possible for Kolya to be so worn down that he confessed to a crime he had never committed? That I cannot understand, whatever you say. And why did they all confess? Because all the women are told that their husbands admitted their guilt. Were they all confused?"

"He simply wasn't able to produce his alibi," Sofia Petrovna said. "You forget, Natasha, how young he still is."

"And why was Alik arrested?"

"Oh, Natasha, if you had only heard the sort of crude remarks he made out loud in the queue. I am quite sure now that Kolya is suffering because of Alik's tongue."

Natasha got ready to leave. As they parted she embraced Sofia Petrovna again and again.

"What's the matter with you today?" Sofia Petrovna asked.

"Nothing, I'm all right . . . Sit down, don't stand up, there's no need. How like Kolya you look, or rather how like you Kolya looks! You will hand the letter in tomorrow, won't you? You won't change your mind?" she asked, looking Sofia Petrovna straight in the eyes. "And don't forget that when they reach F. on the 30th you must without fail hand in some money for Alik – he hasn't got a cent, and his aunt is too scared to hand any in. And then, my dear, I beg you to go and see the doctor. Please! You're just not looking yourself."

"What do I need a doctor for? It's Kolya . . ." Sofia Petrovna said and the tears welled up in her eyes and ran down her cheeks.

Next morning she went to the director's office and silently

laid her letter on the glass top of his desk. Timofeyev read it and, also in silence, nodded his head. Her dismissal had been pushed through with unusual speed. Two hours later it was already displayed on the notice board. In three hours the polite accountant had paid her all she was due. "So you're leaving us? Oh dear, that's not good. Don't forget to drop in to see us; don't forget your old friends."

She walked down the corridor for the last time. "Goodbye," she said to the typists after the bell had rung and they had all banged down the covers of their Underwoods. "All the best!" they all replied in chorus as they had done recently for Natasha, and one of them even came up to Sofia Petrovna and shook her warmly by the hand. Sofia Petrovna was very touched – such a courageous, decent girl! "Good luck!" Erna Semyonovna called out cheerfully, and Sofia Petrovna ceased from that moment to have any doubts that it was Erna Semyonovna and no one else who had written the article.

She went out on to the street, into the noise and bustle of a summer's day. So her working days were over, for ever. She had intended to go home but then decided to visit Natasha. On every corner there were bare-footed boys holding bunches of bluebells and daisies in their sweaty hands. All was well – they were even selling flowers on the street. But because Kolya was in prison or was being transported somewhere by train the whole world had become senseless and beyond her comprehension.

She climbed up – my God, every day it became more difficult to climb those stairs! – and rang the bell. The door was opened by a woman, Natasha's neighbour, who wiped her wet hands on her apron.

"Natalya Sergeyevna was taken to hospital this morning," the woman said in a loud whisper. "She poisoned herself. With veronal. She's in the Mechnikovskaya."

Sofia Petrovna stepped back in surprise. The woman slammed the door.

97

She had to wait a long time for the No. 17 tram. There were two 9s and two 22s but no 17. Then one crept slowly along, stopping for ages at every traffic light. Sofia Petrovna had to stand – even the special seats for passengers with children were occupied, and when a ninth woman with a small child got in nobody wanted to give up a seat. "They'll soon take up the whole tram," an old woman with a stick complained loudly. "They just travel back and forth. We carried our children in our arms. Hold on, you'll be all right!"

Sofia Petrovna's knees were shaking – from fright, from the heat and from the old woman's bad-tempered shouting. At last she got off the tram. For some reason she was convinced that Natasha was already dead. She saw the hospital at once because of the light reflected by all its polished windows. The entrance hall was cool and painted white. She went in and there were three people standing in a queue at the information desk. Sofia Petrovna was not going to jump the queue. A pretty nurse in a starched white smock was dealing with enquiries. By the telephone next to her stood a glass with a bunch of bluebells in it.

"Hello, hello!" she shouted into the telephone after hearing Sofia Petrovna's question. "The second therapeutic ward?" Then, when she had put down the receiver: "Frolenko, Natalya Sergeyevna, died today at four o'clock in the afternoon without having recovered consciousness. Are you a relative? You can have a pass to the mortuary."

15

On the evening of the nineteenth Sofia Petrovna dressed herself in a warm coat, a scarf beneath the coat and galoshes on her feet and took her place in the queue on the embankment. For the first time she was faced with the task of standing in line the whole night without any relief – there was no longer anyone to relieve her. There was no longer any Natasha, no Alik.

Alone Sofia Petrovna had accompanied Natasha's pine coffin all the way across the city to the cemetery. It had been a rainy day, and the big wheel of the cart bearing the coffin had splashed mud into her face.

Natasha was buried in her grave, in the yellow earth, not far from Fyodor Ivanovich. But where were Alik and Kolya? That was something impossible to understand.

She stood on the embankment right through the night, leaning against the cold parapet. The air rising from the Neva was damp and cold. For the first time in her life Sofia Petrovna saw the sun rise. It rose from somewhere beyond the Okhta, and little waves immediately began sweeping along the river, as though someone had stroked it the wrong way.

By morning Sofia Petrovna's legs had gone quite numb from fatigue – there was no feeling in them – and when at nine o'clock the crowd rushed across to the doors of the prison Sofia Petrovna no longer had the strength to run; her legs had become heavy and she felt as though she would have to lift them with her hands in order to move.

Her number this time was 53. After two hours of waiting she

handed the money over at the little window and gave her name. A plump, sleepy man glanced at a card and, instead of the usual "he ain't allowed money", he said "deported". After her interview with Tsvetkov, Sofia Petrovna was fully prepared for this news, though it shocked her just the same.

"Where to?" she asked, half out of her mind.

"He will write to you himself . . . Next!"

She went home on foot, because it was harder for her to stand and wait for a tram than it was to walk. The dust already smelt of the heat, and she unbuttoned her heavy coat and took off her scarf. It seemed to her that the passers-by had forgotten how to walk – they kept bumping into her, sometimes from the front, sometimes from the side.

Kolya would write to her. She would receive other letters like those she had received from Sverdlovsk. Once they had said at the little window that he would write, that meant he *would* write.

For the next few days, without stopping to eat a bite or make her bed, Sofia Petrovna went off first thing in the morning to search for work. The newspapers were full of advertisements saying "Typist needed". Her legs became very swollen but she carried on dutifully all day long, calling at the addresses given. Everywhere she was asked one and the same question: "Has anyone in your family been repressed?"

The first time she didn't understand the question.

"Any relatives been arrested?" they explained.

She was afraid to lie. "My son," she said. It then turned out that the establishment did not have a vacancy. Nowhere could she find one.

She was now afraid of everything and everybody. She was afraid of the cleaner, who looked at her with an indifferent but very stern gaze. She was afraid of the house-manager, who stopped greeting her altogether. (She was no longer the representative of the tenants – the accountant's wife had been

100

elected in her place.) She was very scared of the accountant's wife. She was scared of Valya. She was afraid to go past the publishers. And when she returned home after her fruitless efforts to find a job she was afraid to look at the table in her room in case there was a summons from the police lying on it. Would she be summoned to the police to have her identity card taken away and to be deported? She feared every ring at the door – had they come to confiscate her property?

She was rather afraid to hand in money for Alik. When, one evening on the eve of the 30th she was shuffling along in the queue, Kiparisova came up to her. Kiparisova used to hang around the queue not only on her own day but practically every day, in order to find out from the other women whether there was any news – who had been deported, who was still there and whether there had been any change in the list of names.

"You are wrong to do that, quite wrong!" Kiparisova whispered into Sofia Petrovna's ear when she learnt why Sofia Petrovna was there. "They will link your son's case with that of his friend, and that won't be very good – Article 58–11 – counter-revolutionary organization . . . Why you have to do it I don't understand."

"But they don't ask you who is handing in the money," Sofia Petrovna objected hesitantly. "They only ask who it's for."

Kiparisova took her by the hand and led her away from the crowd.

"They don't have to ask," she said in a whisper. "They know everything." She had huge, brown, exhausted eyes.

Sofia Petrovna went back home.

Next day she didn't leave her bed. She no longer had any reason to get up. She had no desire to get dressed, to pull on her stockings or to step down from the bed. The dust and untidiness in her room no longer bothered her. She didn't care. Nor did she feel hungry. She lay in her bed, thinking of nothing and reading nothing. Novels had long ceased to distract her –

she could not, even for a second, tear herself away from her own life to concentrate her attention on someone else's. Newspapers instilled in her a vague sense of horror. All the words in them were the same as in that number of the wall newspaper *Our Path* . . . From time to time she threw back the blanket and sheet and examined her legs: they were huge and swollen, as if they were full of water.

When the sunlight no longer shone on the wall and evening came, she remembered Natasha's letter. It had been lying all the time beneath her pillow. Sofia Petrovna wanted to read it again and, resting on her elbow, she pulled it out of its envelope.

"Dear Sofia Petrovna, Don't cry over me, there's no one who wants me anyway. For me it's better like this. Perhaps everything will come right and Kolya will be home again, but I haven't got the strength to wait till everything is sorted out. I can't make out what is going on at the present time in the Soviet system. But you carry on living, my dear, and the time will come when it will be possible to send him parcels and he will need you. Send him tins of crab – he loves that. I embrace you with all my strength and thank you for everything as well as for your words at the meeting. I am sorry that you suffered on my account. Let my table-cloth remain with you to remind you of me. Do you remember how we used to go to the cinema together? When Kolya comes back put it on his table – it has got bright colours in it. Tell him that I never believed anything bad about him."

Sofia Petrovna put the letter back under her pillow. But ought she not to tear it up? Natasha wrote about the "present time" in the Soviet system. What if they found the letter? Then they would link Kolya's case with Natasha's . . . or keep it, maybe? After all, Natasha was already dead.

16

Three months passed, and then another three, then it was winter again, January, a year since Kolya's arrest. In a few months it would be a year since Alik was arrested and immediately afterwards the anniversary of Natasha's death.

On the anniversary of Natasha's death Sofia Petrovna would pay a visit to her grave. But on the anniversary of Kolya's arrest there would be nowhere for her to go. His whereabouts were unknown.

There was no letter from Kolya. Five times, even ten times a day Sofia Petrovna would look into the letter-box. Sometimes there were newspapers in it for the accountant's wife or postcards for Valya from her numerous boyfriends, but never a letter for Sofia Petrovna.

After more than a year she still didn't know where he was or what had happened to him. The thought sometimes came to her that the time might come when she wouldn't know whether Kolya was alive or dead.

She had found a job. She was saved from starving to death only by an article by Koltsov in the *Pravda*. A few days after the article appeared – it was a remarkable article about slanderers and people who, afraid to take a stand, caused so much pointless pain to Soviet people – Sofia Petrovna was given a job in a library, not a permanent job, it's true, but still it was a job. She had to write out cards for the catalogue in a special librarian's handwriting – four hours a day, a hundred and twenty roubles a month. In her new job Sofia Petrovna not only did not speak to anyone else – she did not even greet anyone on arriving or leaving. Bent over a desk piled high with books, and wearing spectacles over which her short grey hair fell, she sat out her four hours, then stood up, put the cards together in a pile, took her stick with its rubber tip, which she always had at her side, locked the cards in a cupboard and slowly left the library, looking at no one.

There were tins of crabmeat now stacked up on the window-sill in Sofia Petrovna's room and there were packets of cereals, and still every day after work she set off for the stores to buy up more and more supplies. She bought up tinned foods, butter, dried apples and lard, of which there was plenty in the shops. But when Kolya's letter eventually came one or other of those things might have disappeared from the stores. Sometimes, early in the morning, before getting to work, Sofia Petrovna would go along to the Obvodny, to the flea-market. Haggling fiercely, she would buy a fur hat with ear-flaps or some woollen socks. Then in the evenings she would sit in her untidy and unheated room sewing little sacks and bags out of rags. They would come in handy when it came to sending parcels to Kolya. Boxes made of plywood were poking out from beneath the bed.

She now ate practically nothing – just tea with a slice of bread. She didn't feel like eating and in any case she had no money. The food she was getting ready for the parcels was expensive. For the sake of economy she heated up the stove not more than once a week. For that reason, when she was at home she always wore her old summer coat and mittens. When she felt very cold she would clamber into bed. There was no point in keeping a cold room tidy – it remained cold and uncomfortable just the same – so that Sofia Petrovna no longer swept the floor and wiped the dust only from Kolya's books, from the radio and from the gear-wheel.

As she lay in bed she would turn over in her mind her next letter to Comrade Stalin. She had already written three letters to him since Kolya was arrested. In the first one she asked for Kolya's case to be reviewed and for him to be released because he was not guilty of anything. In the second one she asked to be informed where he was so that she could visit him and see him once more before she died. In the third letter she pleaded to be told just one thing – was he alive or dead. But she received no reply. The first letter she had simply dropped into the post box; the second she registered; with the third she asked for confirmation of delivery. She received the confirmation in a few days. In the place marked "signature of receiver" there was an indecipherable scrawl ending in " . . . yeryan".

Who on earth was this Yeryan? And had he passed the letter to Comrade Stalin? After all, the envelope was marked: "Private and Personal."

Sofia Petrovna went regularly every three months to a legal advice centre. It was quite pleasant chatting with the defence lawyers who were at least polite, not like the Prosecutors. There was a queue to see them as well, but nothing to worry about – not more than an hour or so. Sofia Petrovna would wait patiently, sitting on a chair in the little corridor and resting both hands and her chin on her stick. But her waiting was fruitless. It did not matter which lawyer she spoke to: each one explained to her politely that it was unfortunately impossible to help her son in any way. If his case were to be brought to court, of course, then . . .

On one occasion – it was exactly a year, a month and eleven days since Kolya's arrest – Kiparisova turned up in Sofia Petrovna's room. She entered without knocking and, very out of breath, sank into a chair. Sofia Petrovna eyed her with astonishment – Kiparisova had always been afraid that Ivan Ignatyevich's case might be linked with Kolya's, and for that reason had never called on Sofia Petrovna. Suddenly she had appeared out of the blue.

"They are letting people out," Kiparisova said hoarsely. "I

105

was in the queue just now and I saw with my own eyes – one of the men who have been released came to collect some documents. He wasn't very thin, but his face was very pale. We all gathered round him asking what it was like there. 'Not bad,' he said."

Kiparisova looked at Sofia Petrovna, and Sofia Petrovna looked at Kiparisova.

"Well, I'll be on my way." Kiparisova rose to leave. "I've got a place booked in the queue to see the Prosecutor. No need to see me off, thank you, lest anyone should see us together in the corridor."

So they were letting people out. Some people were being released. They walk out of the iron gates into the street and return home. Now Kolya might be released. A ring at the door and Kolya would walk in. No, there would be a ring at the door and it would be the postman – a telegram from Kolya. Kolya wasn't there; he was far away. He would send a telegram on the way home.

Sofia Petrovna went out on to the stairway and lifted the flap of the letter box. It was empty, nothing in it. For a moment Sofia Petrovna remained staring at the yellow wall, as if hoping that she could conjure a letter out of it.

She had only just returned to her room and threaded a needle (she was making yet another bag) when the door of her room was opened, again without a knock, and the accountant's wife appeared on the threshold along with the house-manager.

Sofia Petrovna stood up, concealing her food store with her body. Neither the nurse nor the house manager greeted her.

"You see!" the nurse started up right away, pointing to the oil-stove and primus. "Just look at it – she's set up a whole kitchen here. Smoke and filth – the whole ceiling is covered. She is destroying the whole house. She won't cook with the others in the kitchen, you see she refuses to, ever since we exposed her for systematically stealing paraffin. Her son's in a camp, condemned as an enemy of the people, and she is without a fixed job herself – in short a doubtful element."

"Citizen Lipatova," said the house-manager, turning to Sofia Petrovna; "you will take this equipment immediately back into the kitchen. Otherwise I shall report you to the police . . ."

With that they left. Sofia Petrovna transported her primus, oil-stove, sieve and saucepans back into the kitchen and put them in their old place. She then lay on her bed and burst into loud sobs. "I can't stand it any more," she said aloud. "I just can't stand any more of it." And again she shouted in a high-pitched voice, with no attempt to restrain herself, syllable by syllable: "I can . . . not . . . stand . . . any . . . more." She pronounced the words so convincingly and so insistently, as though there was somebody standing before her asserting that, on the contrary, she had all that it took to stand even more. "No, I can't, I can't, it is simply impossible for me to take any more."

The policeman's wife came in.

"Don't cry," she whispered, tucking Sofia Petrovna up in a blanket. "Just listen to what I'm saying. They are not acting within the law. My husband says that, since you were not deported, that means no one has the right to turn you out. So don't cry! My husband says that a lot of people are now being released – God grant that Nikolai Fyodorovich will soon be back . . . Valya is getting married and her mother has got her eye on your room. But just don't move, that's all. The mother wants the room for her daughter and the house-manager wants it for his mistress. They will be fighting each other . . . Just don't cry! I'm telling you the truth."

17

In the winter the noise of the street scarcely penetrated into the room through the double windows. But throughout the night Sofia Petrovna could hear rustling and squeaking inside the apartment. The most persistent scratching came from the mice, doing their best to get at the lard bought for Kolya. The floor-boards in the corridor creaked and, when a truck drove by, the front door shook. Every fifteen minutes the clock in the accountant's room solemnly struck the quarter.

Kolya would soon be back. That night Sofia Petrovna no longer had any doubt that Kolya would soon return. Kiparisova had said so and so had the policeman . . . He must return, because if he didn't she would die. If they had started releasing innocent men, that meant Kolya would soon be released. They couldn't release the others and not Kolya. Kolya would return, and then how ashamed the nurse would be! And the house-manager. And Valya. They wouldn't dare to look him in the face. Kolya wouldn't speak to them at all. He would walk past them as if they didn't exist. When he returned he would immediately be given some important job – even a medal – so as to compensate him as quickly as possible for the injury done to him. He would wear a medal on his chest, and he wouldn't condescend to talk to the nurse or to Valya.

Towards morning Sofia Petrovna fell asleep and woke late, at ten o'clock. When she came to herself she remembered – something pleasant had happened the previous day, she had learned something good about Kolya. Yes, that was it – people were beginning to be released from prison. And since they were being released it followed that Kolya would soon be back. And Alik. Everything would be fine, as it had been before. Sofia Petrovna caught herself thinking that Natasha would come back too. No, Natasha would not return, but Kolya would – Kolya might already be on his way home, his train might be drawing into the station.

On her way home that day from the library Sofia Petrovna stopped at a second-hand shop and stood for a long time looking in the window. There was a Leica camera for sale in the window. Kolya had always dreamt of having a camera. It would be a good idea to sell something and buy Kolya the Leica for his birthday. Kolya would very quickly learn how to take pictures – he was so competent and imaginative.

All day long Sofia Petrovna was in an elated, joyful mood. She even had an appetite – the first time for many days. She sat down in the kitchen and began peeling potatoes. If she were to buy Kolya a camera there would then be the problem of where he could develop the films. He would have to have a totally dark room. It would have to be in the store room. The wood was stored there, but they could make room. She could quietly move some of her own wood into the room and ask Degtyarenko's wife to take some into hers – she would not refuse – and there would be enough room. Kolya would take pictures of everybody – Sofia Petrovna, and the twins, and his girlfriends. But he wouldn't photograph the nurse or Valya for love or money. He would build up a whole album of photographs, but Valya and the nurse would never get into it.

"Do you have a lot of wood in the store-room?" Sofia Petrovna asked Degtyarenko's wife when she came into the kitchen for a brush.

"About three bundles," she replied.

"Do you like having your photo taken? I loved it in my young

109

days, at a good photographer's of course . . . Do you know what? Kolya has been released."

"Well now," Degtyarenko's wife exclaimed and dropped her brush. "There you are, and you were in despair!" She kissed Sofia Petrovna on both cheeks. "Did he send a letter or a telegram?"

"A letter. I've just received it. Registered," Sofia replied.

"I didn't hear the postman come. With these primus stoves going you just can't hear a thing."

Sofia Petrovna retired to her room and sat down on the divan. She needed to sit in peace and quiet, to take a rest from talking and to try to understand what she had said. Kolya had been released. They had released Kolya. Her mirror reflected a wrinkled old woman with unkempt grey hair. Would Kolya recognize her when he returned? She went on staring deep into the mirror until everything began to swim before her eyes and she could no longer tell which was the real divan and which the reflection.

"You know, my son has been released. From prison," she told a colleague in the library who was filling in cards at the same table. The woman had until then not heard a single word from Sofia Petrovna, and Sofia Petrovna did not even know her name. But she had to keep repeating her remark, like an incantation.

"Really!" her colleague replied. She was a slovenly, fat woman covered with hairs and the ash from her cigarettes. "Your son was probably not guilty of anything and so he was released. In our country they don't keep a person in gaol for nothing. How long did your son spend in prison?"

"A year and two months."

"So they went into his case again and released him," the fat woman said, putting her cigarette aside and starting to write on her cards.

That evening the policeman Degtyarenko congratulated Sofia Petrovna when he bumped into her in the corridor.

"You owe us a drink," he said shaking her by the hand and smiling broadly. "And when will Nikolai Fyodorovich return to his mama?"

"Oh, he'll put in a couple of months' work at the factory and then he'll go down to the Crimea for a rest – he's in such bad need of a holiday – and then he'll come to me. Or maybe I'll go to him," Sofia Petrovna replied, amazed at the ease with which she said these things.

She was in a state of happy excitement – her legs seemed even to carry her along more quickly. She wanted to keep on saying to someone: "Kolya's been released. Did you know? They've released Kolya." But she had no one to say it to.

In the evening she went down to the shop for bread and ran straight into the polite book-keeper from the publishers. If she had seen him only the day before she would have crossed to the other side of the street, because everything that reminded her of her work in the publishers caused her pain. But now she gave him a friendly smile.

He greeted her very gallantly and asked immediately:

"Have you heard our news? Timofeyev has been arrested."

"What's that?" Sofia Petrovna cried in bewilderment. "But he . . . he's the one who exposed everybody . . . the wreckers."

The book-keeper shrugged his shoulders.

"Now somebody's exposed him . . ."

"I have terribly good news, you know," Sofia Petrovna said hastily. "My son has been released."

"Really? Accept my congratulations. But I didn't know that your son had been arrested."

"Yes, he was, but now he's been released," said Sofia Petrovna happily and said goodbye to the book-keeper.

Returning home she glanced automatically into the letter box. Empty. No letter. Her heart sank, as it always did when she found the box empty. Not a line for a whole year. Had it really been impossible to find someone who could smuggle out a letter? For a year and two months there had not been a word from him. Had he died? Was he still alive?

She lay in her bed and had the feeling that nothing would make her sleep. Then she took a double dose of sleeping tablets. And she fell asleep.

18

"I received another letter today," Sofia Petrovna announced in the kitchen next morning. "Just imagine – the director of the factory has made my son his assistant, his right-hand man. And the local committee has arranged a holiday in the Crimea for him – the countryside is so luxuriant there – I used to go there when I was young. And when he returns he's going to get married. The girl's a young Communist. She's called Ludmila – isn't that a nice name? I shall call her Milochka. She's waited for him a whole year, though she's had lots of other offers. She never believed anything bad of Kolya." Sofia Petrovna glanced triumphantly at the nurse, standing next to her primus. "And now he's going to marry her, as soon as he gets back from the Crimea."

"So you'll have some grandchildren to take care of," said Degtyarenko's wife.

The nurse did not turn a hair. But a minute later, when Sofia Petrovna went to fetch some salt and came back into the kitchen the nurse said "good morning" to her, as though seeing her for the first time. It was the first time she had greeted Sofia Petrovna for a whole year.

Sofia Petrovna had a day off and decided to tidy up her room. If Kolya wasn't yet free, they were bound to release him any minute now. He would arrive and the room would be in such a mess. Glancing at herself in the mirror Sofia Petrovna decided that she simply must start having her hair waved again. Otherwise the strands of grey hair would just hang down. A woman

113

must take care of herself until her dying day. She dragged the boxes out from under the bed and used them to heat the stove. The plywood burnt well, crackling cheerfully. Sofia Petrovna pondered where to store the tins of food so that they weren't piled on the window-sill. What was the point of having so many tins anyway? When they were needed it would always be possible to buy them in the shop.

She decided to clean the windows and the floor. Her legs hurt her as always, and her back was painful, but what could she do – she must put up with it. She tore up the sacks to serve as rags.

While the water was heating she decided to shake out the carpet, so she dragged it out on to the landing. Then she caught sight of something through the cracks in the letter-box. With heavy steps Sofia Petrovna went for the key.

There was a letter lying in the box. The envelope was pink and of poor quality. It was addressed to "Sofia Petrovna Lipatova", written in an unfamiliar hand. There was no address, no postage stamp, nothing.

Forgetting about the carpet on the landing Sofia Petrovna rushed to her room, sat at the window and opened the envelope. Who could it be from?

"Dearest Mum!" The letter was written in Kolya's handwriting and Sofia Petrovna immediately dropped it on to her lap, blinded at the sight of his writing.

"Dearest Mum,

I am alive, and a very kind chap has agreed to deliver this letter to you. How are you getting on? Where is Alik and where is Natalya Sergeyevna? I think all the time of you, my dear ones. It is awful to think that you may now not be living at home but in some other place. All my hopes are now in you, Mum. My sentence was based on evidence given by Sashka Yartsev – you remember, there was a boy of that name in my class. Sashka

114

Yartsev gave evidence that he had drawn me into a terrorist organization. I was forced to confess. But there is no truth in it – we never had any organization. I was beaten up by an interrogator called Yershov who trampled all over me so that I'm almost deaf in one ear. I have sent many appeals from here but none has been answered. Please write in your own name as my elderly mother and set out the facts in a letter. You know very well that I didn't see Sashka Yartsev once after finishing school because he went to a different college. And I was never a friend of his at school. They probably beat him up badly too. Lots of kisses to you and greetings to Alik and Natalya Sergeyevna. Mum, please act quickly, because one can't survive here for long. More kisses,

Your son Kolya."

Sofia Petrovna threw her coat on, pulled her fur hat down over her ears and, still holding a dirty rag, dashed off to see Kiparisova. She was afraid she had forgotten the number of Kiparisova's apartment and that she would not find it. She clutched the letter in her pocket. She hadn't taken her stick with her; she stumbled along, grabbing at the wall. Her legs were letting her down – no matter how she hurried it still seemed a long way to Kiparisova.

At last she reached the entrance to the block and got herself up to the third floor with the last strength in her body. She was right – here it was: "Kiparisova M. E. – one ring."

The door was opened by a little girl who ran away at once. Sofia Petrovna made her way along the dark corridor past the cupboards, opened a door at random and entered.

With her coat on and a stick in her hands Kiparisova was sitting in the middle of the room on a big trunk. The room was completely empty. Not a chair, not a table, no bed and no curtains. Only a telephone on the floor near a window. Sofia Petrovna sat down on the trunk next to the old lady.

115

"I am being deported," Kiparisova said, not at all taken aback at Sofia Petrovna's arrival and without greeting her. "I go tomorrow morning. I've sold everything down to the last thread and I leave tomorrow. My husband has already been deported – for fifteen years. As you see, I have already packed. I've no bed, nothing to sleep on, so I'll sit the night out on my trunk."

Sofia Petrovna handed her Kolya's letter.

Kiparisova took a long time to read it. Then she folded it up and stuffed it into the pocket of Sofia Petrovna's coat.

"Let's go into the bathroom, away from the telephone," she said in a whisper. "When there's a telephone around you can't talk about anything. They have fitted something to the telephone, so that you can't talk on any subject – every word can be picked up at the exchange."

Kiparisova led Sofia Petrovna into the bathroom, put the catch on the door and sat on the edge of the bath. Sofia Petrovna sat next to her.

"Have you already written an appeal?"

"No."

"Then don't write!" Kiparisova whispered, bringing her huge jaundiced eyes close to Sofia Petrovna's face. "Don't write, for the sake of your son. You don't get any prizes for writing that kind of letter. Neither you nor your son. Can you really write that the interrogator beat him up? You mustn't even think of it, let alone write it. They have forgotten to deport you, but if you write such an appeal they'll soon remember. And they'll ship your son even further away. In any case – with whom was the letter sent? Where are the witnesses? How can it be proved?" There was a crazed look in her eyes as she surveyed the bathroom. "No, for goodness' sake don't write anything."

Sofia Petrovna freed her hand, opened the door and left. Slowly she staggered home. She had to lock herself in, sit down and reflect. Should she go to see the Prosecutor Tsvetkov? No. The defence lawyer? No.

She took the letter from her pocket and threw it on the table, took off her coat and sat at the window. It was getting dark and lights were going on in the darkness outside. Spring was on its way, since it became dark so much later. She had to decide, to reflect, but she just sat at the window and thought of nothing. "Dearest Mum . . . I was beaten up by an interrogator called Yershov . . ." Kolya had always had his own way of writing a "D". He had always written like that although, when he was small, Sofia Petrovna had taught him to write "D" the proper way. It was she who had taught him to write, in a lined notebook.

When it was quite dark Sofia Petrovna stood up to turn on the light, but she just couldn't find the switch. Where on earth was the switch? She felt her way along the walls, tripping over the furniture that had been moved for the clear-up. She found it. And her eyes immediately fastened on the letter, crumpled into a ball, glaring at her on the table.

Sofia Petrovna took a match out of the box. She lit the match and set light to the letter from one corner. It curled up and burnt her fingers.

Sofia Petrovna dropped the burning paper on the floor and stamped on it.

Leningrad
November 1939–February 1940

AFTERWORD

[*The best description of what happened to* SOFIA PETROVNA *after it was written appears in Lydia Chukovskaya's book* THE PROCESS OF EXPULSION, *which chronicles her expulsion from the Writers' Union in 1974. This excerpt, translated from the Russian edition published in France in 1979 by YMCA-Press, makes an appropriate afterword to the novella itself. Happily, however, it need not remain the last word. In 1988, nearly fifty years after she wrote* SOFIA PETROVNA, *Lydia Chukovskaya finally got her wish – the book was published in her own country. In February 1988 the novella appeared in the Leningrad literary magazine* NEVA, *prior to its appearance in book form in the Soviet Union as well.* Translator]

In December 1962 fortune truly smiled upon me. The publishing house Sovietski Pisatel (Soviet Writer) signed a contract with me for my beloved book: the novella *Sofia Petrovna*. It is a tale about 1937, written in the winter of 1939–40 after two years of standing in line outside prisons. It's not for me to judge its artistic value, but the value of accurate testimony is indisputable. To this day (1974), I know of no volume of prose about 1937 written in *this* country and at *that* time.

Maybe one exists in some secret hiding place and hasn't yet reached us? Let's hope so . . .

In my novella I tried to show that society had been poisoned by lies as completely as an army might be poisoned by noxious gases. For my heroine I chose not a sister, not a wife, not a

118

sweetheart, not a friend, but that symbol of devotion – a mother. My Sofia Petrovna loses her only son. I wanted to show that when people's lives are deliberately distorted, their feelings become distorted, even maternal ones. Sofia Petrovna is a widow; her son is her life. Kolya is arrested; he is sentenced to hard labour; is called an "enemy of the people". Sofia Petrovna, schooled to believe newspapers and officials more than herself, believes the prosecutor when he tells her that her son has "admitted his crimes" and deserves his sentence, "ten years at hard labour without the right of correspondence". Sofia Petrovna knows full well that Kolya has committed no crime, that he is incapable of it, that to the depths of his being he is loyal to the party, to his factory, to Comrade Stalin personally. But if she is to believe in herself, not in the prosecutor and the newspapers, then . . . then . . . then the universe will collapse, the earth give way beneath her feet, the spiritual comfort in which she has so comfortably lived, worked, rejoiced will turn to dust . . . Sofia Petrovna tries to believe in her son and the prosecutor at the same time, and in the attempt goes mad. (I expressly meant to write a book about society gone mad; poor, mad Sofia Petrovna is no personal heroine; for me she's a personification of those who seriously believed that what took place was rational and just. "We don't imprison people for no reason." Lose that faith, and you're lost; nothing's left but to hang yourself.)

Sofia Petrovna isn't able to generalize from what she sees and experiences; and she's not to be blamed for that, because to the ordinary person what was happening seemed purposely planned senselessness; and how can one make sense of deliberately planned chaos? Particularly when one is all alone: each person was cut off from anyone else experiencing the same thing by a wall of terror. There were many people like Sofia Petrovna, millions, but when people are denied all documents, all litera-ture, when the true history of whole decades is replaced by fictitious history, then the individual intellect is cast back on itself, on its own personal experience, and it works less well than it should.

. . . For years there was only one copy of my novella: a thick school notebook written in lilac ink. I could not keep the notebook at home: I had already been searched three times and had all my belongings confiscated. A friend gave refuge to my notebook. If it had been found in his possession, he would have been drawn and quartered. A month before the war I left Leningrad for Moscow to have an operation; my friend remained in Leningrad; he wasn't drafted into the army for medical reasons and, as I learned later while in evacuation in Tashkent, he died of hunger at the time of the siege. The day before his death, he gave my notebook to his sister: "Give it back to her – if you both survive."

I survived, and my notebook made it back to me. Then Stalin died and the Twentieth Party Congress took place, and I gave my notebook to a typist for copying, and friends of mine read my story. After the Twenty-second Party Congress, in September 1962, I offered my novella to the Sovietski Pisatel publishing house; everything went according to the rules, proper as could be: in December, after two favourable reviews, the novella was approved, accepted, and a contract agreed to; in January 1963 I was paid sixty per cent of my royalty fee; in March I was shown the illustrations already approved by the design department; the manuscript was on the verge of going to press and becoming a book.

Miraculous!

I saw that the publishers were well disposed towards my book, sympathetic to it and to me. The young women editors wept when they read it, and every one asked for a copy to take to mother or husband; the artist completed her illustrations with uncommon speed. So much for the artist! Comrade Karpova herself, the chief editor, the right hand of the director,

Comrade Lesuchevsky, that very Karpova from whom up to now in my literary career I'd had nothing but polite crudeness, now addressed me with nothing but crude compliments.

The only thing the publishers asked of me was to write a foreword. I wrote one.

The compliments lavished upon me both sincere and insincere were most understandable. And so also the speed with which my book was read, reviewed, and prepared for press. And why not! After all the "cult of personality" had been unmasked, Stalin's body removed from the mausoleum and every newspaper, every magazine, every publishing house was obliged to "respond" at least in some degree to "the exposure of the mass infractions of soviet legality" – with an article, a short story, some poetry, a novella, or a novel.

They responded! Karpova, sighing deeply and sympathetically, spoke of the tragic past, unmasked in so wise and timely a fashion by the party – a past that would never return, and of the "restoration of Leninist norms to party life". (As if those norms had been religiously observed in non-party life all along.)

Then suddenly – some sensed it earlier, I, distinctly, in 1963 – everywhere, ever-increasing, worrisome rumours began to spread: there'd been a change of course "at the top", dissatisfaction, literature was digging too deeply into the "consequences of the cult", it was time to talk of achievements, not "mistakes"; the party with its decisions at the Twentieth and Twenty-second Congresses had explained and corrected everything; enough is enough. The survivors returning from camps and prisons had been rehabilitated, and not only given housing but, just think of it, provided with jobs; the relatives of those who died had been informed of the posthumous rehabilitation of sons, sisters, husbands; what more did you want? why pour salt on the wounds? let's get on with the latest planting or the latest harvest. "At factory X there's a new blast furnace."

On 7 and 8 March 1963 explanatory meetings with party and

government leaders were held for the intelligentsia. I was not high up enough in the intelligentsia to be invited to such exalted meetings; but in May I received a different sort of invitation, to my publishing house. The head of the department of Soviet literature, Comrade Kozlov, invited me to his office and with apparent friendliness but categorical firmness explained that though accepted, ready for press, and even sixty per cent paid for, my novella could not be published.

I wanted to drop in on Karpova upon learning this, but she wasn't there: either she was sick, on holiday, or away on business. I don't remember.

Certainly, the decision not to publish my book was a personal disaster, a cause for grief, but I didn't hold the publishing house to blame. I saw that many of the people who worked there sincerely wanted to publish my novella. After all in our country (in cases of any importance), it's not the editors who decide what to publish or not publish. An order's an order, a forbidden topic's a forbidden topic . . . However, after a while I did drop in on my book's chief admirer, the main editor of Sovietski Pisatel, Comrade Karpova. I took a seat in an armchair across from her. Did she think, I asked, that the prohibition would last a long time.

"It's strange," I said by the way. "It's like making a decision to publish three novellas, three narrative poems, three short stories, three novels about the Great Patriotic War* – full stop. 'We're not going to pour salt on the wounds!' But after all every family lost either father, or husband, or brother, or son, and sometimes four people in one family were killed, and it's painful for relatives to remember those who perished. The war lasted four years, but 'the cult of personality' and its 'consequences', almost thirty. In each family all trace of father, or husband, or brother, or wife, or sister, or sometimes the whole family itself

* The Russian name for World War II. (Translator)

has disappeared. The war was a terrible thing, but one can understand the reasons for it, the idea behind it, but understanding the idea and reasons for 'the cult of personality', and everything this 'cult' gave rise to, is much more difficult. So every document is precious for future generations, for researchers, my novella included."

"From the very start," Karpova answered as if by rote, "I told you your novella was ideologically flawed. The reasons for and consequences of the cult have been adequately explained by the publication of party documents in the papers. The speeches of Nikita Sergeevich and the meetings for the intelligentsia with party and government leaders have further clarified things. I was never mistaken about the flaws in your position."

Karpova, the chief editor of Sovietski Pisatel publishing house, was famous and is still famous in literary circles for her pathological dishonesty. "To lie like Karpova" became proverbial long ago. But meeting a direct, bold, shameless lie, no matter how often it happens, always stuns one anew. Karpova had never uttered a single word about my book being ideologically defective. Quite the contrary, she more than anyone had hastened to sign the contract and announce the "approval" of the book.

"You should be ashamed of yourself," I burst out.

"Be grateful," Karpova answered, pointing to some papers, "that the publishing house has not demanded its money back. It's a waste to spend government money on your novella."

(Government money! It wasn't for money I wrote my book at a time when all around me in my beloved city every tenth person was being shot, maybe every fifth.)

However, the liar had given me a wonderful thought. The idea for a way to strike back.

"The money?" I asked, getting to my feet. "You don't have the right to ask me to give the money back. It's against the law. A manuscript which has been accepted and readied for publication must be paid for in full. It's not I who owe you money, but you who owe me. I'm going to take the matter to court. The publishing house changed its mind? Then let it pay the penalty, what's the author got to do with it?"

"Just go ahead and try," answered Karpova to my retreating back.

After a time I went to the lawyer for the Writers' Union. When he heard that my manuscript had been approved and accepted, that the illustrations had been done, and that I'd been paid sixty per cent of my fee, he determined that I definitely had grounds to sue. But he added: "Writers usually don't sue their publishing houses because the publisher will stop publishing them." That didn't bother me. I went to the Office for the Protection of Authors' Rights where one of the young lawyers, upon acquainting himself with the contract, immediately agreed to prepare a suit on my behalf and to represent me in court.

The time before the trial passed slowly. The judge called me and asked for the manuscript. It took him a month to read it, if not longer. He didn't express any opinion. Then the court date was twice set and twice set aside: the defendant didn't appear. On purpose: or so it seemed to me. Finally, on 24 April 1965, an open session of the People's Court of the Sverdlovsk Region of the city of Moscow took place. The small hall was filled. The judge handled the affair drily and precisely, as before saying nothing about the novella. The lawyer for Sovietski Pisatel publishing house was very longwinded. He informed the judge that the novella was found to contain "ideological distortion", that at first the publishing house employees, "due to an over-zealous response to the Twentieth and Twenty-second Party Congresses", had not noticed the distortion, but now in the light of the new party decisions, "they had looked at the novella with fresh eyes"; that my novella was no more than a photograph of the ugly side of our life; material of the sort which could be used to produce only "a work which struck at clear party positions"; that the novella was ideologically inadequate; that after the publication of *One Day in the Life of Ivan Denisovich* the publishing house had been swamped by a torrent of prison camp books which had to be limited; and as to Solzhenitsyn, he could assure us that no one was about to publish him again. "Yes, yes, he's getting ready to do so, but we're not . . ." "We ourselves didn't realize the danger of the theme, but it was pointed out to us it's not necessary for Communists to publish books on this theme, and even more important, it's not useful . . ." There was laughter and whispering in the courtroom, and I noticed that many people were taking notes.* "If Chukovskaya wins this case," concluded the lawyer for the Writers' Union, "it will set a bad precedent." The lawyer from Protection of Authors' Rights, on the other hand, was very brief. He noted that we were not in England, that legal proceedings in our country were not based on precedent, but the law as to authors' rights was clear (he cited the relevant points): since the manuscript had been approved for publication, the publishing house was obliged, no matter what, to pay the author the full fee.

The courtroom listened to him sympathetically, the judge, without emotion.

A few times, after one of the speeches by the longwinded lawyer for the publishing house, the judge instructed me: "Answer!"

I answered. I said, in part, that if they stopped publishing Solzhenitsyn it would be a great shame for the country; that, incidentally, my *Sofia Petrovna* and his *Ivan Denisovich* were novellas written at different times, about different times, and on different themes: his was about the camps, mine, about "ordinary life"; I also said that if my novella had been accepted

---

* Not long ago I learned that one of the transcripts of these proceedings was published abroad in 1972 – seven years later – in *Political Diary*, pp. 51–57. (Author)

and readied for press "in an overzealous response to the Twentieth and Twenty-second Congress", then hadn't the contract been broken due to an overzealous response to the new moment? And was it possible that the decisions of the Twentieth and Twenty-second Congresses were simply "an overzealous response . . ." and nothing more? I said that if the evil done in the past had occurred, wasn't it largely because newspaper editors, snowed under by groaning, weeping, wailing letters in which families beseeched them to investigate the cases of their relatives, had been denied the possibility of printing those letters? The editors were not able to satisfy the demands of the moment. And truly, who at that time "dared to dare"? To print such a wail would have meant printing your own death warrant.

Wasn't one of the reasons it could happen, the readiness of all editors, across our whole enormous country, the editors of all newspapers, books, magazines, always to obey the baton of the conductor standing on the podium as to whether to permit some piece of information or other on the pages of his publication (for example, news of illegal arrest and torture)? I said: granted my novella may be only a photograph, not a great painting, but caught on this photograph is a moment of enormous importance to our society, and the novella is essential to all those who wish to think about what took place.

The court assessors* questioned the defendant, mainly clarifying the dates of "the passage of events". The judge was silent. Essentially, he asked the lawyer for the publishing house only one question. Granting him the opportunity to substantiate his assertion that my novella was "ideologically defective", the judge asked:

"Is it true that when the manuscript was approved for

---

* Two civilians who, together with the judge, hear cases in a Soviet court and serve as jury in the determination of the verdict. (Translator)

publication and the author was paid sixty per cent of her fee the novella was satisfactory?"

Having listened to the lawyer for the publishing house, to the lawyer from "Protection of Authors' Rights" and to me, the court withdrew to deliberate.

Twenty minutes passed:

"The judge enters . . . All rise . . ."

In cautious anticipation, the courtroom rose.

"In the name of the Federated Russian Soviet Socialist Republic . . ."

In the name of the Russian Republic the People's Court of the Sverdlovsk region resolved: the publishing house must pay the author the entire royalty fee since the manuscript had been rejected after it had been approved for publication.

In a few days I received the money . . .

As to the novella?

Courts have no jurisdiction over the publishing of books.

The novella, snapped up by Samizdat long before and travelling hand-to-hand, crossed the border.

In 1965 in Paris the novella was published in Russian by Five Continents Publishers under a different name (*The Deserted House*) and with changed names for many of the characters as well (for instance Olga Petrovna instead of Sofia Petrovna). Then it was published in America, also in Russian, in two issues of *Novy Zhurnal* (New Journal, Nos. 83 & 84, New York, 1966) under the correct title and without changed names. Then it seems it was translated into many of the world's languages: with my own eyes I have seen it in English, in German, in Dutch, in Swedish and have heard that there are editions in still other languages.

I am grateful to Samizdat, to the foreign publishers and translators. No random search in connection with case No. 27 or 227 or 20227 can now destroy my testimony. Certainly it was wrong to give my novella a different title (*The Deserted House*

127

instead of the name of the heroine); my book deals with an educated society driven to loss of consciousness by lies. Sofia Petrovna (Olga Petrovna also) represents this society. The change of title in this case is an attempt to change the basic idea . . . But for all that, I'm still grateful.

However, despite my gratitude, I'm not consoled. There's only one thing I want, just one thing I'm waiting for: to see my book published in the Soviet Union.

In my own country. In Sofia Petrovna's country.

I have been waiting patiently for thirty-four years.

There is but one tribunal to which I wish to offer my novella: that of my countrymen, young and old, particularly the old, those who lived through the same thing which befell me and that woman so different from me whom I chose as the heroine of my narrative – Sofia Petrovna, one of thousands I saw all about me.